MAX'S CAMPERVAN

PICKLED IN THE Pub

TYLER RHODES

Copyright © 2024 Tyler Rhodes

Dedicated to everyone who bought a horrendously expensive cast-iron pan. It's an investment!

Chapter 1

"I'm beat," sighed Min, my ex-wife, love of my life, and the prettiest woman any utterly unbiased, adoring ex-chef had ever seen.

Anxious whined from the grass beside her as she kicked off her Converse and wiggled her red-painted toes. The exhausted Jack Russell Terrier opened a lazy eye, gave her big toe a half-hearted lick, then groaned before he curled up tight and began to snore.

"I think we broke Anxious," I chuckled, sinking into the camping chair beside Min and slipping out of my Crocs. Say what you will about plastic clogs, they beat any other form of footwear when you're mooching about in a field or wandering along the beach.

Min took the offered Prosecco with a warm smile and we clinked glasses.

"Cheers," I said.

"Cheers."

As the afternoon sun beat down, we took a sip of the bubbly booze.

"That is so good. Thanks for coming."

"It was my pleasure. Thanks for such a lovely day out. That was a lot of walking though. I feel like I've run a marathon. Portmeirion was amazing, and it's so clever how the different pieces of architecture have been arranged. I loved how they painted windows on the side of buildings to make it look like they were real."

"It sure was a cool place. I'm glad we got an early start, so now we have the whole evening ahead of us."

"Yes, and we get to be here for your weird pickle festival. I can't believe we're staying in a pub car park and watching people get excited about pickled onions. Look at them. It's beyond strange."

"People love pickles," I shrugged, unable to stop a manic grin creeping across my face. I lifted my hand to rub at my beard which had grown in nicely now, sprinkled with grey like my long hair. Min reckoned it brought out the intensity of my eyes, and made me look like a wild man of the mountain, but in a good way, so I vowed to go with it and enjoy the freedom not having a job entailed. And I was loving this vanlife!

"There better not be any murders!" warned Min. "And why are you looking so creepy? You need to stop smiling. It's really odd."

"No, it isn't," I laughed, taking another sip of wine.

"Max, it so is." Min's face lit up as she was unable to contain her smile. "I'm happy."

"Me too. And Min?"

"Yes?"

"I'm glad you're happy. I'm relieved we're still best friends, and pleased you decided to come and stay for the day. And night, I hope." I wiggled my eyebrows suggestively, knowing what the answer would be, but you can't blame a man for trying.

"Yes, for the night, but you're in the weird bed up by the pop-up roof. No funny business."

"I can wait."

"Good, because you'll have a long wait. Friends, remember? We talked about this, and you know I still love you, but we've only been divorced a year. We need time to find ourselves. Ensure this is what we really want."

"You mean sitting outside pubs drinking Prosecco while we wait to sample pickled onions?"

"Yes, something like that," she grumbled, her eyes twinkling as she brushed a wayward lock of sun-bleached blond hair from her tanned face. "Let me look at the flyer again, and are you sure we don't have to pay to stay here?"

"I told you, I have a book full of places to stay for free. I pay a yearly subscription to be a member, then I can just rock up and spend a night or two. Lots of pubs do it, and plenty of tourist attractions, even a few places along the coast too. We're a bit inland now, but I thought a country pub would make a nice change from the beach. I didn't expect it to be quite so cool though."

"It is beautiful here. Old pub, large beer garden, trees, a river, and a perfect spot to park the campervan for a few nights. It's stunning."

We took a moment to appreciate our luck. When I'd arrived, I assumed there had been a mistake, expecting to stay in a grotty car park and just take advantage of the fact that Portmeirion in Gwynedd, North Wales was only twenty minutes away. It came as a pleasant surprise to discover that I could stay beside the pub with just a few other motorhomes there, and basically crawl from my camping chair to one of the picnic benches.

The fact there was to be a pickled onion festival this evening was a total shock, with stalls, food on offer in the pub, a live folk band later on, and even a pickled onion eating competition to be held after hours. Odd, verging on mad, but it sounded like fun. If nothing else, I was intrigued.

The pub fronted a wide expanse of grass that led to the river, with trees shading the water from the early evening sun. We'd taken a stroll down there when we got back from our day trip, but the lure of a chair and a glass of wine was too tempting. Plus, we wanted to watch the festival take shape.

"I've never seen anything like this in my life," said Min, shaking her head in astonishment.

"Me either," I admitted. "In my time as a chef I went to all kinds of farmers markets, food festivals, harvest festivals, fruit and veg shows, competitions, and the list goes on, but I've never heard of a pickled onion festival."

"I think festival is too strong a word for it." Min laughed as she pointed at the extent of the celebrations. "There are a few gazebos, a ticket stall, two or three people selling jars of onions, and a bloke demonstrating how to pickle them. Not exactly a massive event."

"Not even a small event. More like a non-event. But the bloke who runs the pub, Ronnie, said they've been doing it for five years and the crowds get bigger every year."

"By crowds, do you mean that bloke with the dog?"

I turned to follow the slow amble of an old fella being dragged along by his overweight Labrador. He wore a flat cap, loose blue corduroys, and a faded chequered shirt with the sleeves rolled up to reveal tanned forearms and strong hands. He was the only one there apart from those setting up the gazebos and the lucky dip, but the stallholders chatted happily and there was a definite buzz of excitement in the air.

"Maybe it'll pick up later."

"Then there might be two men with dogs! Ooh, can't wait!" Min winked, then sipped her wine.

We were having the time of our lives, and it was certainly novel. Some people thought it strange that we remained such close friends, others thought it cute, so sweet, and adorable. They didn't understand in the slightest.

I'd screwed up in a monumental way and put being a top chef above our relationship, but when everything came crashing down I'd realised my mistake and done my best to rectify the damage. It was an ongoing process and one I would never stop repairing, but what we'd both realised once the dust had settled was that we genuinely loved each other.

Maybe that wasn't enough for us to rebuild our previous life, but it didn't stop us building a different one. Often apart, but like all best friends we spoke and saw each other regularly. As I'd explained to Min mere days ago, there was no hurry. We both needed time to become our own person without the other, and we had decades left on this planet. So we'd decided to cruise along and absolutely not rush into anything intimate for fear of ruining what we currently had. I just wished she wasn't so damn sexy!

"You look hot," I blurted, unable to help myself.

"The wine's cooling me down. But this weather is crazy, right?"

"Um, yes, absolutely," I agreed, grinning because I'd got away with it.

"I know what you meant, silly. And thank you. You look good too. You've slimmed down even more, and your tan is awesome."

"I've been doing my workouts at least five times a week. Anxious and I were overindulging at the start of our adventure, but we've reined it in. He's not too happy about it, but he needs to stay in shape too."

"It looks like they're ready." Min indicated the festival with a nod.

"This is so weird," I chuckled.

We watched in awe and astonishment as Ronnie—looking like a bank robber more than a pub landlord—exited the pub, the hinges creaking as the tiny double doors banged shut, a pair of scissors held aloft like a grand prize.

Proud as any new parent, he took his time walking the short distance to the field where the gazebos and stalls were now set up. The three men and one woman manning the entire festival stood in a line next to a red ribbon tied to two poles while the old guy with the dog waited to one side, wiping his nose with a handkerchief, looking bored. The dog lay down by his feet and licked at its nethers.

"Hey, you guys coming to the grand opening?" asked Stu, his wife Harper hanging on his suntanned arm. They were the other couple in a large motorhome staying in the free camping spot, and were lovely, if rather keen on the intricacies of just about everything.

"Wouldn't miss it for the world," I said, heaving out of my chair. I turned to Min, offered my hand, and asked,

"Would m'lady care to join us for the opening of the pickled onion festival?"

Grinning, Min put her glass on the small camping coffee table I'd bought off Amazon and got delivered to the pub—so cool you could do that—and allowed me to haul her to her feet, then said, "I'd be delighted."

With a nod to Stu and Harper, the four of us walked arm in arm across the car park, onto the grass, and stood beside the old guy. His dog lifted its head, farted, then jumped in surprise at the noisy emanation before standing and snapping to attention as people waited with bated breath.

"I now declare the sixth annual pickled onion festival of The Dead Crow officially open!" Ronnie beamed with pride as he cut the ribbon, then bowed as the applause rang out.

Feeling like we should add to the meagre reception, Min and I cheered, but were beaten by several decibels as Stu and Harper clapped vigorously, beaming at us.

"We come every year," confided Stu. "We were even here for the first one."

"Is that right?" I asked, somehow managing to keep a straight face.

"Oh yes," gushed Harper. "We didn't even know it was on, but it was such fun that now we make a point of coming back every year. It's part of our yearly list of must-see things. Never a dull moment with this vanlife, eh?"

"No, never," I agreed, ignoring Min as she nudged me in the ribs and I noted her shaking with hardly restrained mirth.

Ronnie the landlord, a solidly built, bald-headed block of a man with gangster written all over him, although he spoke softly but with a hint of a cockney accent, smiled at us and said, "Thank you everyone for comin'. It's lovely to see some new faces, and Stu and Harper, it's always a pleasure. As you're here before the festival really gets started, I want to offer you the usual bonus. Don't tell anyone," he said, checking there were no eavesdroppers—there were no anything—"but we're having our usual lock-in after hours, so be sure to stick around for that." He winked, then beamed at us, waiting for our reply.

"You know we love a lock-in," said Stu, rubbing his hands together.

"Do you mean drinking after the pub is shut?" asked Min.

"Yes, my dear. It's tradition. Nobody minds as long as we keep it relatively quiet, so we have a few extra drinks, on the house of course, once it's past closing time. You're all welcome. And don't forget we do the pickled onion eating competition then too."

"Thanks, Ronnie, that's very kind of you," I said. "There's a band too?"

"Oh yeah, Freaky Fiddlers are amazing! They'll be here soon. They have a motorhome they use to travel around, although the lads live in the village. They always draw a large crowd."

"Even larger than for the opening?" asked Min, quaking so much she was ready to burst.

"Now, young lady, no need for sarcasm. Usually there are hundreds for the festival, but there was an accident on the main route and the coaches and cars got delayed. But you wait."

As if on cue, a horn sounded and we turned to watch a coach weave its way around the corner of the narrow country lane and pull into the car park.

"Told you," crowed Ronnie, beaming. With a nod, he hurried over.

"There's another one!" gasped Min.

"And look how many cars there are!" I said, astonished.

"I told you both earlier, this place rocks for the festival," said Stu as he tugged at his faded Motorhead T-shirt clinging to his large belly, his deep tan making his shock of thinning white hair look silver.

"This is the highlight of the year," squealed Harper.

They were so alike it was disconcerting. Both had a head of white hair down to their shoulders, wrists festooned with festival bands, leather bracelets, and mementos from their travels, and the same bright blue eyes. They wore matching straw hats, band T-shirts, and cut-off jeans like me. I wondered if this was what I'd look like in a few decades. They were lovely people, very upbeat, keen on life, and adored their vanlife. The lucky pair had taken early retirement five years ago and had been living in their impressive motorhome ever since, surviving frugally off the rental income from their old house.

Keen on festivals of all sorts, I'd heard about the music they enjoyed—old rockers—the food they preferred —traditional British—and their love of the sun. It was an idyllic life and they loved to chat.

Before we knew it, we were swamped by about as mixed a crowd as you could imagine. The coaches contained the pearl and perm brigade. Elderly ladies from various women's groups keen for an onion-themed day out. The other coach was from several local pensioner groups with a mixed bag of eager elderly gents and less than enamoured people tagging along as it beat sitting in a chair all day.

But as the car park filled with day trippers, it became evident that the pickled onion festival had a reputation amongst the younger crowd too. Grinning and laughing, from what I overheard as they headed for the gazebos, this was a rather ironic outing that they found amusing, bizarre, and downright peculiar. But in a fun, generous-of-spirit kind of way.

"Look, they're setting up more stuff now," said Min with a nudge.

"Wow! Where did that all come from?"

"From the coaches, and the cars. They have cake. And is that a cheese stall?"

"It is! And pies. And what's that?"

Unable to resist the fantastic aromas drifting our way, and with Anxious already weaving between legs after being utterly disinterested so far, we followed our noses and mingled with what was now a large and very animated group come to celebrate *The Dead Crow Pickled Onion Fest.*

Ronnie was in his element, lording it up, loud and red-faced as he brimmed with pride and extolled the virtues of the pickled onion to anyone who would listen and quite a few who wouldn't.

Suddenly, his already red face turned beetroot and he gasped as his eyes rolled up and he staggered.

"Oh no, not again," I groaned as I tugged Min through the throng after him.

"You said there would be no deaths," she hissed as we hurried to Ronnie.

"Quick, do something!" shouted Stu as he and Harper caught up with us.

"Ronnie, what's happened?" I shouted above the din.

He clutched his chest, wheezed, pulled a jar of pickled onions from behind his back, then grinned like a maniac and declared, "I think I was on my way to pickled onion Heaven!" The manic landlord cracked the jar, upended the contents into his hands, then threw the tiny onions into the air and belted out, "Let's get this party started!"

People cheered, I sighed in relief, and Min laughed nervously as everyone tried to catch the onions falling like well-preserved biblical rain down on a crowd of people outside a pub in the middle of Wales to celebrate what actually was turning out to be a rather entertaining day.

"And nobody died," said Min, shaking her head in wonder at me.

"You had to go and spoil it, didn't you?" I grumbled.

"What? I was just saying."

"Just remember what you said when it all goes pear-shaped."

"Don't be daft. It's about onions, not murder."

"Yes, sorry. It's just after the last few times it's becoming rather a regular occurrence."

"Max, relax. Here, have an onion."

Min handed over one she'd caught. I bit into it and crunched the tiny vegetable in half. Incredibly tart vinegar squirted to the back of my throat, making me cough and splutter.

"Let's get our onions on!" I shouted, and everyone went wild.

A more bizarre evening I have yet to experience.

Chapter 2

"Why do they hold it so late in the day?" asked Min as we took a moment to escape the throng and stood at the edge of the festivities.

"Ronnie was telling me all about it yesterday and said it's because it means it won't rain."

"How would he know that?"

I shrugged. "I have no idea. He reckons that if you do it in the afternoon it will rain, but whoever heard of a pickle festival getting rained off in the early evening?"

"He has a point," conceded Min. "But that's only because nobody else has ever heard of a pickled onion festival at all."

"I think this is one of those things where you just have to go with it and have a good time. Come on, let's go and see what there is to buy."

We took it slow, with Anxious now back with us, and perused the various offerings. Min bought cheese, I bought bread and two pies for tomorrow, and despite our vow not to get suckered in by the onions, we both emerged from the throng of keen shoppers an hour later weighed down with more jars of onions in pickling solutions than I had ever imagined were available.

"Stupid onions," I muttered, annoyed with myself for getting carried away.

"Your breath will stink for the next year," Min teased as we lay out our wares on the outdoor kitchen table I'd set up under the sun shelter.

We stood back and studied the neat row of jars, then laughed.

"What are we going to do with all this?" I asked. "I mean, you have to take half, obviously, but it's still a lot of onions."

"I'm not taking half! I don't even really like them."

"Then why did you buy so many?"

"It seemed rude not to. Everyone went to so much trouble, and I think I got caught up in the excitement." Min put a hand to her mouth and breathed into it then sniffed. "Ugh, that stinks! Does it really smell that bad?" She leaned forward and exhaled right into my face and I staggered back, overwhelmed by the fumes.

"That's pretty intense. How about me?" I huffed a breath and Min almost collapsed. I grabbed her and grinned as her colour rose and her eyes began to stream with a ready flow of tears.

"That is beyond strong. I think we could breathe fire if you have any matches to light it."

"You know what they say," I admonished. "Only fools eat pickled onions and play with matches."

Our wine was still where we left it, so we downed our tepid drinks quickly, topped them up with a cold one from the fridge, and sank into our chairs to take the weight off. It had been a very long day after our outing, and yet we were both buzzing from the peculiar events still raging on the grass.

Ronnie the landlord was milling about by the entrance, shielding his eyes as he looked for someone or something. His frown deepened as he clearly came up short, then spied us and hurried over, repeatedly checking the people coming and going.

"Have you seen Dexter?"

"Who's that?" I asked. "Are you okay?"

"Sure. Um, no. Yeah, I mean. Sorry, I'm all flustered. Damn donkey has disappeared and he's needed."

"Donkey? You're looking for a donkey?" asked Min.

"No, I meant he's a donkey. An annoying idiot. He's the chef, and we're getting a ton of orders piling up ready for later, but he's nowhere to be seen. The kitchen's already short-staffed as the waitress didn't turn up, but we'll manage. But without the chef it'll be a disaster."

"What does he look like?" I asked.

"Bloke in a big white hat and an apron," Ronnie shrugged. "You can't exactly miss him."

"Without the hat and apron?" I hinted.

"Oh, yeah, sorry. Big guy, ginger hair, rosy cheeks. Basically, think of a chef, and that's what he looks like."

"Max is a chef and he doesn't look like that," blurted Min.

I tried to melt her with the power of my gaze, but she just smiled warmly and shrugged.

"You're a chef?" gushed Ronnie, his plan written all over his face.

"Strictly retired. I used to work in Michelin 3-star restaurants but gave it up to get my life together and live in the van."

"That's awesome. And I'm guessing you're the ex-wife?" he asked Min.

"Ronnie and I had a chat yesterday and I told him you were coming," I explained.

"Yes, pleased to meet you. It's Ronnie, right? I'm Min."

They exchanged a handshake then Ronnie asked, "Think you could help me out, Max? Just for a few hours. We serve strictly between seven and nine today. It's late, I know, but we make a killing because of the onions and the limited time slot. After that, it's party time and drinks will be on the house. I'll pay, too, obviously, whatever you want." Ronnie thought for a moment, then added, "As long as it's just the regular wage I always pay. Please? Help a bloke out here?"

"You should do it, Max," said Min, smiling her encouragement.

"I don't want to fall into my old ways," I admitted. "You know how I was. It's why I packed it in. I was going to put something on for our dinner soon. Another one-pot wonder. It's my thing," I explained to Ronnie.

"Have yourself a nice steak from the kitchen after you finish," he suggested. "We have some incredible sirloin, and it's local meat. Best there is. Please. Go on, mate. Just this once?"

"Will there be pickled onions?" I asked warily.

"Of course! Loads."

"Great, just great," I groaned, heaving to my sore feet and glaring at Min. Then I smiled, and I saw her understanding dawn as she shook her head, but I turned to Ronnie and said, "Actually, Min used to be a waitress many years ago. I bet she still knows how. She always said how much she enjoyed waiting tables and talking to customers. And with all that onion breath going around today, it'll be a real treat for her."

Min hissed in disgust at me, but was laughing as she said, "Yes, fine, I'll help too. But two hours tops, then I want a nice drink."

"Deal."

Keen to get going, Ronnie said he'd meet us inside. I asked about Anxious and he said he'd be fine in the pub but not the kitchen, which Min was happy about.

We changed into some more suitable clothes, meaning, I put my Crocs back on and Min emerged from the camper looking like a goddess.

"How did you manage to do your hair, brush your teeth, apply make-up, and get changed in five minutes?" I asked, astonished, as I'd only just managed to get my clogs on.

"The lure of a free drink and a fun night serving people food even though I want to just sit and do nothing," she grumbled, but with unmistakable excitement in her eyes.

"You want to do this, don't you?"

"Maybe. Actually, yes. I've been a dietitian for years, so doing something like this will be fun. A change. And I promise not to judge what everyone orders."

"Good, because this is a traditional pub, so I expect it will be fish and chips, pie and chips, chips and chips, or double chips and chips."

"I saw the menu, and they call them fries. You can get cheesy fries, double fries, thick fries, or—"

"Thick fries are chips. Only thin chips are called fries," I lectured.

"—burger and fries." Min finished with a smile, then laughed. "Come on, we don't want to be late for our first day of work."

"Make that first and last," I reminded her.

The interior was heaving with the elderly crowd drinking tea and raving about onions, the younger groups sampling local ales and cajoling each other about their breath. Most tables were already taken, with plenty of customers standing at the bar. It was a proper "olde worlde" British country pub with a flagstone floor and dark beams holding a sagging yellow ceiling. Every available inch of wall space was festooned with pictures of the local area, photos of the pub through the ages, and an awful lot of rosettes.

The bar had a brass rail, gleaming pumps, and offered a wide array of local cask ales and ciders. Ronnie was in his element pulling pints and giving the customers the banter, but when he saw us he rushed over.

"You're both life-savers. Min, I'll show you our system, which is basically ask people what they want, write it on a pad, then take it to the kitchen if it's for food. Max, you come with me. I'll show you around the kitchen and introduce you to Meat."

"To meet who?"

"No, the other guy in the kitchen. He's called Meat, as in, um, Meat."

"Okay," I said warily, not sure I fancied working with someone called Meat. Was this someone from Ronnie's past? A gangster turned chef who got his nickname by chopping people up and serving them with roast potatoes? I hoped not, for obvious reasons.

Reticent to return to a commercial kitchen, even if it was in a pub called The Dead Crow, I was surprised to find I had butterflies in my stomach as I followed Ronnie through the back down a corridor, then into the kitchen.

The sights, smells, and sounds of the kitchen were as familiar to me as my own voice, and my heart leapt as I stepped inside. This was exactly what I'd been afraid of, and why I'd had to go cold turkey on work for fear of getting drawn back into this world within a world known to so few. Loved and hated in equal measure by those lucky enough to gain access to this sacred environment.

"Not a bad set-up," I whistled, eyeing up the industrial gas stove, the various ovens, the stainless steel counters and shelves, and the well-organised layout for the prep area.

"Thanks. We do a lot of food most days, but the weekends are incredible. Today is actually a quieter day because we only do a few hours this evening. We'd usually serve in the afternoon, too, but I like to focus on the onions."

I studied Ronnie for a twitch or a smile, but there was nothing but sincerity behind his hard eyes. What was his game? He didn't seem the type to be found in rural Wales running a country pub. More like he should be in the East End running a boozer for other geezers and dabbling in a bit of armed robbery between pint-pulling.

"It's well-stocked and the layout's good. I'm not too keen on the brand of oven, but I can cope for today. Show me where everything is and what system you use, and who does what here?"

"You're top chef. Meat does whatever needs doing. That's it."

"That's it? Nobody else?" I asked, surprised.

"Nope. Why, how many people do you usually have in a kitchen?"

"About fifteen. Maybe ten if it's a smaller place."

"Then you're in for a treat," beamed Ronnie, seemingly immune to reality. "Nice and quiet for you. I appreciate this, Max, and Ronnie doesn't forget his friends, if you get my drift."

I didn't, and I certainly never asked what he meant. "Let's do this."

I was led to the grill and there I met what could only be described as muscle with a mouth. A man with no neck, shoulders wider than he was tall, forearms thick with veins, and sweating badly through his crew-cut. His apron was already covered in gravy, he had a wild look in his eyes like he was ready to run at the slightest provocation, and he was absolutely butchering the cod.

"Max, meet Meat. Meat, meet Max," said Ronnie without a trace of amusement.

"Hi."

"Alright, Max." Meat and I shook. Surprisingly for a buff dude obsessed with the weights, and no doubt copious amounts of illegal growth hormone, his handshake was firm but not overly so. He knew he was strong and didn't show off about it.

"Here, let me," I said as I placed my hand carefully over his as he tried to fillet the fish like a blind man in a room full of ghosts whilst being threatened with disembowelment.

"Yeah, sure. Thanks. Ronnie, I ain't used to this pressure. It's no good for my heart. You know I'm not a leader. I wanna just do my thing and not have any stress."

"Then you're in luck."

"You found Dexter?"

"No, but when I do he'll get what for. This is Max, a real chef. 3-star posh and all that. He's taking over for today, so you can go back to... er, what do you do?"

"I make the gravy, watch the ovens, sort the veg, and do the dishes," grumbled Meat as he wiped the sweat from his wrinkled brow.

"Course you do," chortled Ronnie with a slap on Meat's wide back. Ronnie winced as he lifted his hand and looked at it suspiciously.

"So, you guys go way back together, I'm guessing?" I asked as I filleted the fish in a few deft slices even with a less than optimal knife.

"How did you know?" asked Ronnie. "We came up together in London and around those parts. When I called it quits and moved here, Meat tagged along as he'd had enough of the old life too. Been here for what, seven years now?"

"Yeah, seven. We like it. No bother, no trouble. Just drinks, grub, old dears, and the occasional band. And the onions. Lovely stuff." Meat reached over to a jar and forked an onion then crunched happily.

"So, what did you guys do down south?"

"A bit of this, a bit of that. Ducking and diving. Bouncers at clubs, some security, whatever. Neither of us were well-behaved at school and we were always off getting up to no good, but we always worked, brought home the bacon, and have been lifelong buddies." Ronnie beamed at Meat, his friend smiled back warmly, and there was obviously a real connection there.

"No wives?" I asked.

"Divorced, just like you," grinned Ronnie.

"Hey, welcome to the club," said Meat as he popped another onion in.

"Max is different to us, Meat. He's got his bird with him. She's a right looker and she's filling in out front right now. They're together but not together, if you know what I mean?"

"Nope," he said cheerily.

"We're just friends, but one day we'll be a couple again," I explained.

"Good for you."

"Right, I'll leave you to it," said Ronnie. "Meat will sort you out with everything you need. The orders come through over there," Ronnie pointed to the serving counter, "and hopefully Dexter will turn up soon anyway. Where can he be?"

"You know what's he's like, Ronnie. He's probably gone off for a smoke and fallen over like the dumb idiot he is. Remember the other week when he got lost for the whole afternoon? He only went out to get some fresh air as it was so hot, and he didn't come back till it was dark."

"Yeah, he's not the best with directions," grumbled Ronnie. But then he smiled, turned about sharpish, and was gone.

The next few hours flew by in a flurry of activity. Despite my misgivings, Meat was a seasoned pro in the kitchen if kept away from the fish, and we functioned well as a team. He worked hard, was continually washing dishes if not doing anything else, and kept a spotless kitchen in general. Surfaces were wiped immediately, pans placed at the ready for me, orders called on time, and we settled into a routine so familiar that I spent the entire time in a dreamlike state of blissful ignorance of the world outside. I didn't once think of Min, or Anxious, or anything else, and it was only when the last order had been called and I was wiping down the counters that I came back to myself.

It was absolutely awful. I felt physically sick with the realisation of how easily I'd slipped back into a role I'd assumed I would never take on again. I hated that I could become so all-consumed and not give a second thought to how either Min or Anxious were faring just the other side of the wall. Was Anxious okay out there? How was Min coping? No, I'd completely dismissed them from my entire existence, and although there was nothing wrong with being focused on the job at hand, I knew I should have at least checked on them.

I vowed that this was the last time I would enter a commercial kitchen, even a pub one, as it wasn't good for my head or those I cherished most in this world. But there was no denying that I'd enjoyed myself immensely, and the familiar sights, sounds, and smells followed me as I went to the back door to dispose of the bin full of rubbish we'd made during our few hours of intense action.

The cooler air hit with a shock, and I hadn't even realised how sweaty and boiling I was until I stepped out into the night. Dusk had come and gone, night was truly here, and I stood, soaking in the stillness of a perfect June evening, the bag of rubbish in my hand forgotten. I breathed deeply to centre myself, to bring myself under control and to activate my brain again after being so lost to my old passion.

It simply wasn't worth it. I was too single-minded, too obsessive, and too involved to ever be able to do this for a living again. What I also realised was that although I had enjoyed it immensely, I preferred to be out here in the real world, not stuck inside where everything else was forgotten. I had made the right choice. Vanlife was better for my mental health, my soul, my loved ones.

Nodding and smiling, I wandered over to the large commercial bin then paused when I heard a sound. A muffled cry for help? Tentatively, I lifted the lid, expecting the worst, but a cat hissed, glared at me like it was my fault, then was gone into the night.

Laughing with relief, I flung the bag into the bin, shut the lid properly, and headed back inside.

Meat was still busy with the dishes, so I figured I'd help finish up and opened the door to the broom closet as I watched him work efficiently and with no wasted movement. It was like spying on the Terminator while he did household chores.

Shaking my head in wonder, I turned back to the now open door and shrieked as a large man teetered, his eyes open, staring at nothing, his face rigid, the skin a peculiar green tinge. Bile and bits of onion had dribbled from his open mouth down his otherwise pristine chef's whites.

Momentum taking over, he reeled forward and slammed into me, sending me crashing to the hard floor.

Guess I'd found the missing chef.

Chapter 3

"Meat! Meat!"

Heeding my call, he lumbered over and heaved the corpse off me; the sour smell of onions remained. Clambering to my feet in a panic, I stood, transfixed by the sight of Meat cradling the body like a baby, not a very overweight, very dead chef. He placed the man on the floor then grunted.

His eyes slowly tracked up from the body to me, and he asked, "You okay?"

"I think so. Damn, he was heavy."

"He was fat, and you're a better chef."

"Thanks."

We both studied Dexter, a weird stillness in the eye of the storm.

"He smells bad."

"He sure does. This is definitely the chef?"

"Yeah. Dexter. Used to be Dangerous Dex, but that was in the old days."

"Right, of course. Don't know how I could forget that. Dexter's dead. He was in the broom closet. Didn't anyone look in there?"

"Why would they?" Meat shrugged, seemingly unmoved by the corpse at our feet.

"Fair point. I suppose everything was already out where we needed it. I just wanted a mop."

"I'll get it."

Meat stepped over the body to enter the broom closet, but I said, "Wait! I don't need it now. We should do something about him."

"Uh, yeah, sure." Meat wandered off, leaving me alone with Dexter. Another of Ronnie's cronies, I assumed, but it was weird how little Meat seemed bothered by the death of a friend. I checked in the cupboard, wondering why he'd been in there with the door closed, why he had remained upright, and why this kept happening to me. Everything was neat and orderly, but very cramped, and with Dexter in there he'd have basically filled up the entire space.

My guess was that he'd simply not had room to move and had slumped forward against the door, waiting for it to be opened. I noticed the bloody splodge where his face had rested against the door, the unmistakable pungent aroma of onions still strong in the room. On a shelf there was a half-finished open jar of the onions, and that explained why it stank in here, but why was the jar in the broom closet, and more importantly, why was Dexter?

I stepped out just as Meat and Ronnie returned. Ronnie looked angry, Meat looked just like Meat always did. Rather bewildered by the world in general.

"You weren't winding me up," noted Ronnie with a grunt as he stared down at the deceased chef.

"Told you."

We were motionless as we studied Dexter. A tear fell from Ronnie's eye, and he said, "Goodbye, Dexter my old mucker. I'll miss you."

"Take it easy, brother," said Meat, sniffling.

Neither man showed any more emotion, their faces now blank, and I wasn't sure if he was an old crony or not, so I asked, "Did Dexter come here with you guys too?"

"Yeah, he's been around for like ever. Part of the gang. Shame he's gone." Ronnie shook himself out and added, "I guess it happens to us all eventually. We'll see him right."

"You aren't upset?" I asked.

"Course, but we've seen our fair share of death over the years, right, Meat?"

"Loads. It's why we're here. To get away from that nonsense. It ain't good for the soul."

"True," said Ronnie, shaking his head. "Poor Dexter. He was such a fun guy. Always joking around. I told him not to eat any more onions, though, and it looks like the daft bugger choked on one."

"He hid in the broom closet to eat onions?" I asked.

"He's done it a few times. Not with onions, not since last year anyway, but my guess is he was stuffing his face. I totally forgot about him hiding there."

"Me too," said Meat, tutting. "Daft sod. What a way to go."

"Nasty," agreed Ronnie. "But at least he went out doing what he loved best. Eating."

They seemed to find this hilarious and were soon laughing so hard they were bent double. When they'd finished, they wiped their eyes, grunted, and their faces became slack again.

"I don't get how you can be laughing one moment, devoid of emotion the next."

"It's how we are. It's the way we're wired. In case you hadn't noticed, Max, we're not your usual country pub kinda guys. We're from the city, from the streets, used to a hard life and harder men. Wait, that came out wrong," said Ronnie, holding a hand up. "I mean, we knew hard men. Real hard. No, still wrong. We knew tough guys, saw plenty get taken out, and we'd all had enough. We love it here, and Dexter was in his element. But we all gotta go, and he went out how he wanted. End of."

"End of," agreed Meat.

"What now?" I asked.

"Now? Now we stuff him in the freezer, pretend like it didn't happen, go have a party, and sort this out in the morning."

"You're joking, right? We need to call the police. They need to come and investigate. Forensics, the coroner's office, detectives, the whole works."

"Not tonight they don't. And besides, there's no phone signal. And the internet's down and we don't have a landline any more. So what can we do?"

"You're making that up, aren't you?"

"What if I am?" laughed Ronnie, but his eyes never left mine and he said more with a look that he ever could with words.

"Okay, I get it. You don't want to ruin the night. You have a lot of people in, I assume?"

"A fair few, and it will get busier later. In half an hour or so when everyone arrives for the music. We need the cash, Max, so don't go blabbing to everyone about this and ruining it for me. Cops tomorrow. Tonight, we party. It's what Dexter would have wanted."

"He did love a party," agreed Meat.

"What if it wasn't an accident?" I asked. "I've been involved in a few murders lately and helped solve them, and what if this is another one?"

"Max, our old life was left behind years ago. Dexter choked on an onion because he was a greedy bugger and gobbling grub in the broom closet. Case closed. Relax. But why were you involved in murder investigations? You aren't a cop, are you?"

They bristled and stepped forward. No easy task with Dexter between us.

"No, I'm an ex-chef, remember? But I got caught up in a few things and figured out who committed the crimes."

"Then we're all good, Max. If it was murder, you can figure it out this evening and we can tell the cops in the morning when they arrive. But tonight you keep schtum, are we clear?"

"Okay, if you think that's for the best. It's your place."

"It is. Now, go wash up and let's go have us a ball."

"We should call the police," grunted Meat.

We both gawped at him. I knew why I was, because it was so unexpected, but Ronnie was even more dumbfounded.

"Are you nuts? That's the last thing we need."

"Dexter was our friend. We all came up together and he deserves to be treated right. What if it was something dodgy?"

"Dodgy? He was stuffing his face in the broom closet. There's a jar of onions in there. It's dodgy, but only insofar as he was obsessed with food. This will put a right damper on the whole night. They'll probably shut us down."

"Why would we get shut down? He choked, or had a heart attack, or whatever. An ambulance will arrive, but we can tell them to come in without any lights flashing, nip round the back, and nobody will be any the wiser. He was our mate."

Ronnie glanced from me to Meat, then we looked at Dexter lying on the kitchen floor. "Fine, I'll call, but don't say I didn't warn you. What do you think will happen? Seriously? A couple of dodgy geezers running a boozer and one of them is dead? The cops will be all over this like a nasty rash."

"Mate, you got it all wrong. Your head's been stuck in the sand. The emergency services are snowed under because of the weather, and they ain't exactly speedy even when it isn't a mad rush. There aren't enough ambulances or police to go round. Call them, and I bet they won't even come tonight."

"Let's step out the back and find out," sighed Ronnie.

"You're doing the right thing," I said, smiling at Meat for standing up to Ronnie. "Your friend deserves to be treated properly."

"Fine." Ronnie grunted, then stepped over Dexter and we trailed after him out into the beer garden.

Quite a few revellers were enjoying the space and cooler air, so we moved to a quiet spot and Ronnie fished out his phone. "Give me space here, guys," he hissed as we crowded around. He moved off into the dark then called emergency services and asked for an ambulance. He explained where we were, that a man had been found dead, most likely having choked or suffered a heart attack, and answered several questions, including that he'd confirmed the man was dead.

"That the best you can do?" he asked. "Fine, if you say so." A long pause. "No, 1 understand." Another pause. "Yes, we do." A final pause. "Thanks." Ronnie jabbed at his phone then pocketed it.

"How long will they be?" asked Meat.

Ronnie joined us and sighed. "They said the ambulances in the area are overrun as usual and that even if this was an emergency the current wait time could be a few hours. Because this isn't an emergency and I said I was definitely sure Meat was dead, they might not get to us until the early hours of the morning, if then."

"What about police?" I asked.

"Same. Busy because of the heat. People keeling over with sunstroke, lots of other stuff going on." He shrugged. "They said someone might come out, but maybe not. They didn't seem too bothered, and I said we had somewhere we could put him. So, looks like the party's back on, guys. Good news, eh?"

"Sweet," gushed Meat.

Both men rubbed their hands together and I could almost see the money signs behind their eyes. I guess running a country pub wasn't the most lucrative of businesses and they wanted to take advantage of the custom when they could.

"So, where are we going to put him?" I asked.

"That, my friend," beamed Ronnie as he slapped my back, "won't be a problem."

Back inside, I stared at Ronnie and Meat, aghast. "You can't be serious?"

"Deadly," growled Ronnie. Then he smiled warmly and said, "It's perfect. We aren't serving food now, there's plenty of room, and it will keep the meat fresh. Geddit?" he chortled.

"Ah, good one, Ronnie," laughed Meat. "It's funny because it's my name."

Ronnie rolled his eyes. "Yes, well done, Meat."

"But it's the freezer. For meat," I protested.

"It ain't for me," said Meat.

"No, I meant to keep the meat you eat in."

"We'll just drag him in there and lay him on the floor. He won't contaminate stuff as he isn't touching anything. We can wrap him up if you think that will help?"

"I... But... Let me think for a moment." In all my years as a chef, I'd never encountered this particular type of problem before, but I was certain it went against every health and safety rule there was. But then again, it wasn't my business, it wasn't my food I was risking, and I assumed that if we did wrap him up nothing would actually be tainted. He'd cool down, sure, but I doubted he'd be frozen solid by the morning or whenever the emergency services arrived. Maybe they'd arrive sooner than anticipated and he'd just be taken out and that would be the end of it. Whatever happened, it wasn't up to me.

"Well?" asked Ronnie, tapping his foot.

"Okay, let's do it. But this is weird. You know that, don't you?"

"Mate, putting a corpse in a freezer isn't as weird as you might think," laughed Ronnie.

"He's right," agreed Meat with a sinister chuckle as he cracked his knuckles.

We returned to the kitchen and the two gangsters expertly managed to get a tarpaulin underneath the bulk of Dexter by turning him first one way then the other. We dragged the tarp into the walk-in freezer and both men wrapped up their friend and even tied the ends in a matter of seconds.

I tried not to think about how easy they'd made it seem, and that they'd most likely had plenty of practice at such activities. I was beyond relieved when both men stood and turned to me and Ronnie said, "Fancy a pint?"

"I really do," I admitted. "Like you wouldn't believe."

"Me too. That was a busy evening," said Meat. "Poor Dexter."

"Poor Dexter," agreed Ronnie. "But the show must go on. That's what he'd want."

"He would. Dexter loved the pickled onion festival and he loved folk music, so let's get out there and see him off in style."

"Not a word to anyone," warned Ronnie. "You can tell your missus if you must, but I do not want to hear anyone talking about this. Got it?"

"Sure, Ronnie, whatever you say."

After they left, I removed my apron, had a thorough wash, took a deep breath, then plastered a smile on my face and tried to forget about what had happened. I paused before I headed into the pub and tried to think things through, and came to the conclusion that maybe this was for the best. After all, Dexter was dead, and there was nothing anyone could do about that.

If the ambulances were busy trying to save people's lives, then surely it was better for them to do that than chase out here into the middle of nowhere to collect a body? I'd heard lots of stories over the previous few years about how understaffed and overworked the National Health Service was, but over the last few weeks whenever there had been a death they always arrived promptly, and faster than I'd expected. But that was when we were closer to main towns, and often it had still taken an hour or two for the ambulance to arrive and for teams to assemble.

But that was for murder, and surely this was nothing of the sort? Just a guy who'd taken his food obsession one step too far.

So why didn't this feel right?

Was I overlooking something and there was more to this than I'd first thought? Knowing I'd be antsy all night if I didn't check, I returned to the broom closet and opened the door. The smell of pickling vinegar was strong, even overpowering the chemical cleaners lined up in matching containers, but the room was neat and well-organised, nothing odd to see apart from the jar of onions on the shelf.

The label was missing, which I thought strange, but then lots of people had been involved in making their own, so maybe this was a jar Dexter had made himself last year and thought he'd sample now it had matured. Or was it from one of the stalls, or hadn't there been lots of jars being given away for free to people too? Yes, and we'd been given one just like this along with plenty of other people.

Generic jars to get people interested, then they could buy from the stallholders who had their own labels to indicate the brand and exactly what kind of vinegar infused onion you would be consuming.

With nothing to see, and no reason to suspect foul play, I decided that there really was nothing to be done and Dexter had just died in a very unfortunate way.

Time to go let my hair down and check on Min and Anxious. After only a few hours apart, I missed them.

Chapter 4

"Oh my god, what is happening?" I asked Min as I found her sitting on a stool at the bar, a half empty glass of wine in front of her.

"Don't ask," she grumbled, wincing as she bent her leg and rubbed her foot, her shoes on the floor.

Anxious whined and pawed at my legs so I bent and made a fuss of him; his tail thumped against me as he groaned in happiness.

"Did you behave yourself?" I asked as I ruffled his back.

He barked happily, grinning like we'd been apart for days.

"Sorry to leave you, but I had to help out the landlord. And Ronnie isn't the kind of guy you say no to."

"He seems a real sweetie," said Min as I straightened and she slid a pint of something cold and bubbly towards me.

"Thanks. What is it? No, don't tell me, because I don't care." I took a sip and sighed, let my shoulders relax, and slid onto an empty stool so our knees almost touched. "That's good. What an evening. How did you cope?"

"It was kind of fun, but exhausting. I can't believe you got me into being a waitress. You sneak." Min smiled, but she looked tired and ready for bed.

"Hey, you forced me into the kitchen, so I think you deserved to suffer too. But what's going on here?"

We turned to watch the press of bodies trying to squeeze through the doors at the same time. Canes were raised, grumbles were loud, and jars of pickled onions were held aloft.

"The coach party is leaving. There's a curfew at the retirement home, and the Women's Institute aren't fans of the music. They just came for the onions and the cheap food."

"Right. So, it went okay out here?"

"Yes, everyone was very sweet. Some of those old fellas are a bit handsy though. They haven't heard that we aren't in the sixties anymore and you can't go groping bums just because you're a pensioner."

"I bet you gave them a few harsh words," I laughed.

"You can count on it. But it was fun, and Anxious was a dear. Everyone loved him, and I don't think we need to worry about his dinner. He ate more than anyone else."

At the mention of his name, Anxious launched onto my lap, barely making it, and plopped down with a grumble.

"Blimey! He feels twice as heavy. I think we should take him outside for a while to get some air and have a pee. Fancy a wander to cool down? It's boiling in here. And I need to have a word with you anyway."

"Anything wrong?"

"I hope not, but I'm not sure."

The coach parties had left now, leaving a younger crowd mixed with what I assumed were regulars and a few stalwart onion fans staying for the entertainment. The band was setting up in a corner of the pub over by the large log burner, not that it was on as it was stifling inside and the windows were streaming with condensation.

Ronnie and Meat were doing the rounds, chatting to people, checking on the musicians, both looking in their element. Ronnie paused by a group of three men in a corner booth who were neither smiling nor eating onions. Three pints were placed before them by the barmaid, and they grunted their thanks then started talking to Ronnie, serious expressions on their faces. Cronies of his, I assumed.

I let Anxious down, then he followed Min and me outside into the fresh air. We paused while the coach lights lit up the pub before they turned and were gone, leaving us blinking until our eyes adjusted.

"Let's wander down towards the water. The lights are strong enough to see."

"Sure." Min laced her arm through mine and I felt instantly calmer.

We moved away from the noise and bright lights of the pub and into the shelter of the trees. Lit from the pub, they cast long shadows across the water, but it felt safe here and I wondered if the same could be said of the pub.

"Min, I have to tell you something, and I don't want you to freak out."

"Okay. But you're freaking me out already."

"You remember the chef, Dexter, who was missing?"

"Yes."

"I found him."

"That's nice."

"No, it isn't. He was in the broom closet. I opened the door and he toppled onto me. The guy's dead, Min. Stone cold dead."

"That's awful! Are you alright? Was it gross?"

"Kinda gross. I'm fine, but a little shaken. He'd been eating onions."

"Onions? I don't understand."

"Apparently, he was food-obsessed and would hide so he could eat. Ronnie said he forgot that Dexter had been discovered in the cupboard before, so didn't look. There was an open jar of pickled onions in there and he'd choked by the looks of it. There were bits of onion and blood down his shirt and apron, and he fell on top of me. He weighed a ton."

"That poor man. What did Ronnie say?"

"See, this is where it gets weird. There's this other guy, too, Meat."

"He's a dear. I spoke to him earlier."

"I wouldn't call him a dear, but that's not important now. He's like Ronnie, a bit of a geezer. They're clearly ex-gangster types and go way back. All three of them did. But neither of them were cut up about Dexter. They took it in their stride and didn't want to call the police or ask for an ambulance until tomorrow. They thought it would ruin the night."

"It definitely would, but what else can you do?"

"They wanted to leave him in the freezer. It's a large walk-in type. Actually, that's what we've done."

"Max, what are you talking about? You can't do that! The ambulance will be here soon."

"No, Ronnie called them, but he took some convincing, and they can't come until the morning most likely. They're snowed under and said this isn't an emergency so we're right at the bottom of the list. Same for the police. They might or might not send someone out, but it could be hours. Even up on the coast it took ages for the services to arrive at the campsite, and the same when we found the other body. It was different on the beach because there were people in the area, but out here things are super slow and my guess is they have other things to do."

"I suppose that makes sense when there's no sign of foul play and somebody just dies." Min frowned as she tugged at my arm and asked, "You don't think Ronnie or this Meat guy had anything to do with it?"

"I really don't know. Like I said, neither were exactly despairing, but they were sad he was gone. It's not wanting to call the authorities that has me worried. I understand they need the business, but some things are more important than money."

"Max, that's true, and I know your heart is in the right place, but don't forget it's easy to say that when you have enough. If they're struggling to earn a living here, then a day like today is important for them. Not just the business they'll miss out on tonight, but the fact word will get around and people won't want to come next year. If they leave it until tomorrow, nobody will ever know the chef died like that."

"True, and I agree, but I'm not sure we're safe here. Maybe we should leave."

"We can't leave. You'll have to give a statement to the police because you found the body. And where would we go?"

"Anywhere away from here. Min, they're gangsters, and there are some dodgy looking blokes in the pub too."

"There are always dodgy blokes in pubs. And you said it yourself, Ronnie's an ex-gangster. I think it's sweet that he's turned his life around. He's obviously not on the run or anything and seems like a nice man. He even gave me a bonus for my work." Min beamed, cheeks flushed, and was clearly having a good time.

"Okay," I relented, "if you're sure? I don't want to put you in any danger. You know how it goes lately. There might be more to this than meets the eye."

"Max, you're becoming obsessed. I know there have been a few unfortunate incidents, but people do just die, you know?"

"I know. It's just... I'm not sure, but after the other times I suppose I'm thinking the worst and that somebody might have done it on purpose."

"Force-fed a man in a broom closet onions?" she taunted. "Sorry, I didn't mean to make fun. But lighten up. I'm sorry you found him, but relax. Enjoy the evening. The music's about to start, so let's enjoy ourselves, have a few drinks, and worry about this in the morning."

"Maybe you're right. Maybe I'm being suspicious because of the last few times. Come on, you can buy me a drink with your wages."

"No need," Min gloated. "Ronnie said drinks were on the house, remember? And have you eaten?"

"No, I haven't, and I am starving."

"Me too. You going to knock me up something tasty?"

I groaned, but knew I could handle a few more minutes in the kitchen. "Follow me," I said, feeling smug.

"What's your game?" Min put a hand to her hip and studied me with her head cocked.

"You'll see."

Ten minutes later, I was trying to resist shouting at Min as she turned the steaks for the fifth time. You were meant to fry them once either side and be done! Why was she fiddling? And had she checked on the chips?

I managed to keep it together while she plated up and actually enjoyed my overcooked steak because at that moment there was nowhere I'd rather be than sitting in the beer garden with Min and Anxious, the music from the pub drifting out on the cool evening air.

When we were finished, we cleared up in the kitchen then returned to the front-of-house as the music got into full swing.

The place was packed. Freaky Fiddlers were kicking up a storm with the three-piece trio clearly enjoying themselves as much as the crowd. Dressed in flat caps, farm shirts, jeans, and boots, with thick beards and long hair, they clearly knew their stuff and the instrument playing was hypnotic, the vocals pitch-perfect.

People were dancing, weaving around each other and locking arms then moving on to the next person, everyone grinning, singing along, and thoroughly having fun. Hipsters sang the choruses, grizzled farmer types banged their glasses on the table, elderly couples nodded to the rhythm, and Ronnie and Meat were at the centre of things, jumping around, arms swinging with abandon, not a care in the world. In fact, they seemed to be celebrating.

Min and I got fresh drinks and Anxious coped well with the noise even though it wasn't really his thing. But the offerings of crisps and the occasional pickled onion were enough to ensure he enjoyed himself. He did the rounds of the tables, getting made a fuss of, much to his delight. Nothing like a trapped audience to get more ear scratches than one dog could handle.

It wasn't long before my worries of earlier were forgotten as we got caught up in the moment, and our exhaustion vanished as the merriment increased. We danced, we sang, we shouted very loudly, and had the best time ever.

When the music finally finished, Min and I slumped into a corner booth, utterly exhausted but grinning and happy. Anxious pawed at my legs, clearly as tired as us, so I lifted him up and he settled between us, relieved the music was over and he could get some much-needed rest. He was snoring almost immediately, and I knew he'd stay that way until morning if we let him.

"That was fun," gasped Min, her cheeks rosy, face glistening.

"It sure was. I haven't danced like that for years. I'm done for."

"Me too. But it was worth it. It's been a great day, Max. Thank you."

"You're welcome. It was my pleasure. And I appreciate you coming."

"Don't say it like I was doing you a favour. I wanted to come. I love seeing you and Anxious. Will you look at him?" Min's face lit up like it always did as we both studied our little dog, his whiskers twitching, whimpering as he dreamed of giving the elusive rabbits what for and finally catching one.

"I don't mean it like that. I'm just glad you came. I think Anxious is glad too."

Min laughed. "Of course he is. I'm awesome!"

"Fancy another drink?"

"Why not? I could happily crawl into bed, but I'm having the best time."

I nodded, then made my way to the bar as the crowd thinned now the music was over. Plenty of people were leaving as it was getting late. The band had overrun and it was close to last orders now, so those who remained were hurrying to get a drink in.

Tanya the barmaid served me, her grey vest showcasing full sleeves of tattoos. The shaved sides of her head, and long, silky black hair tied back in a scruffy bun made her look menacing and dangerous, but she had a warm smile, rosy cheeks, and was very polite.

"Anything else, Max?" she asked with a wink.

"No, I'm good, thanks. You doing okay? It's been a busy night."

"I prefer it like this. Makes the time go faster. And I know the guys from the band, so it's always good to see them."

"No trouble?"

"Trouble? Why do you ask?"

"Your arm. The bruise." My eyes lingered on the purple and yellow bruise on her upper arm, then shifted to meet her gaze when she looked up.

"It's nothing. I just tripped. Gave it a right wallop on the door frame." She shrugged it off and smiled.

"At least it wasn't more serious. But I'm glad you're okay."

"Thanks for asking, but it's only a bump."

"And what about those guys?" I glanced over at the three gangster types still sitting at the table, fresh pints raised as they spoke quietly to each other, none of them smiling. "They don't seem the folk music type."

Tanya chuckled as she slid the drinks across the spotless counter. "Don't worry about those sweethearts. They're pussycats. Just some of Ronnie's old crew, but they're past doing anything dodgy. One of them runs a florists, the other two are a couple." Tanya leaned forward, eyes glinting with mischief as she whispered, "They kept it a secret when they were criminals back in the day, but now they're all lovey dovey and run a B&B a few miles away."

"How come the whole crowd moved into rural Wales? Why up here?"

"Because it's a long way from London and far enough away from the old life. They've been out of the game for years, so don't stress about it. Ronnie, Meat, and Dexter are good guys. Ronnie owns the place but the other two work here and he pays them well. I think Ronnie was the boss back in the day, so looks after his guys. The three at the table are always in here, and although they look grumpy they've never been any bother. You get used to it." Tanya shrugged, then turned to a waiting customer and asked, "Yes, love, what'll it be?"

I snuck a glance at the three men again, who were now laughing and smiling as they spoke. I'd just assumed the worst from a few brief glances, but of course not everyone spends their whole life grinning like an idiot.

Fears eased, I took the drinks back over to Min to find she'd been joined by Stu and Harper, the retired heavy metal and music festival fans, who were clearly having a great time judging by their rosy glows and their animated hands.

"Hi. Can I get you both a drink while I'm up?" I asked.

"No thanks, we've still got ours, and there's no hurry," said Stu, grinning.

"That's right," squealed Harper. "Ronnie always has a lock-in after the pickled onion festival. Would you like one?" Harper offered the jar after taking an onion for herself with a fork.

"I'll pass. If I eat another onion I think I'll turn into one."

"You can never have enough," laughed Stu.

"You definitely can," said Harper. "And your breath means you've had plenty." Harper wafted in front of her face then pinched her nose.

"It does smell very ripe in here," chortled Stu, "or is that just me?" He burst into a fit of laughter, clearly finding it highly amusing.

Min and I exchanged a surprised glance, but they were just in high spirits. I settled next to Anxious so we were opposite our guests, and noted several more people leave just as Ronnie rang a bell and shouted, "Last orders, ladies and gents. Ten minutes, then it's time."

"Time for what?" shouted Meat with a roar of laughter following.

"Time for you layabouts to go home. You had your onions, you've eaten our grub, swilled our beer, and now it's time to hit the hay."

"Come on, Ronnie, we all know that's not going to happen," one of Ronnie's old buddies shouted.

Ronnie shook his head and glared at him then took in the room, clearly checking who was here and who might tell on him if he let people stay after hours.

Everyone quietened down after that, and soon enough Ronnie called time. Most of the remaining customers left, unaware there was to be a lock-in or too tired to consider more drinks and an even later night.

Chapter 5

Ronnie saw the last of the customers out, closed the doors, slid the bolts across with a rather ominous thud, and turned, face creased in a nasty scowl as he surveyed the remaining clientele. Then his face split into a wide grin and he growled, "Right, you 'orrible lot, let's get this party started!"

With cheers from the remaining stalwarts, a quick blast on the fiddle from the band, and raucous thuds on the table, which was seemingly what you did when you realised you were one of the select few chosen to be part of the lock-in, Ronnie, Meat, and Tanya did the rounds of the tables and cubbies. They took people's orders, refusing any money, just suggesting we put whatever we felt was fair in a charity box for the local dog rescue centre and the tip jar for Tanya.

By the way the money flowed from the hands of some, both the dogs and Tanya could retire to Barbados the following morning.

"Did you see how much that old farmer put in?" I gasped.

"That's no farmer," noted Stu in a whisper. "That's Giant Graham."

Min and I both turned to watch as Giant Graham had a few words with Ronnie whilst slipping what looked like another twenty into Tanya's tip jar.

"He doesn't look very big," said Min.

"He isn't. That's why they call him Giant. It's ironic. Don't mention his size to him. I heard that back in the day Graham once chopped a bloke's legs off for saying he was short."

"That's just a silly rumour," scolded Harper, brushing her hand through her silver hair and waving at Graham who waved back, smiling.

"It isn't. A bloke told me."

"Oh, so a bloke told you, did he? Then it must be true."

"Is this place just full of gangsters and old cronies of Ronnie's then?" I asked.

"No, just a few. We have the crowd of three who live around here, then there's Graham, and I think that's about it. A few years back there were more of them. They'd all make the trip up from London for the festival, but it's eased off as Ronnie broke more ties with the old crowd. He prefers it like this. In fact, he'd rather it if none of them came, but they aren't the type of men you tell to stay away."

"How do you know so much about it?" I asked.

"I hear things. We get around."

"And Ronnie told you last year," said Harper, shaking her head.

"Yeah, that too," Stu mumbled, grinning at us.

Anxious whimpered in his sleep and everyone aahed, a sound impossible not to make when there's a dog being cute.

"He's so lovely," said Harper. "What was his name again?"

"It's Anxious, remember?" said Stu.

"Of course! How silly of me." Harper giggled, then asked Stu, "Want to dance?"

"How could I resist an invitation from such a lovely lady?" Stu stood, held out his hand, and Harper took it. As they walked over to the band playing quietly, he pinched her bum and she turned, giggling, then pecked him on the cheek.

"They're a lovely couple," said Min, beaming.

"They sure are. And both love their life of freedom."

"Like you."

"Sure, like me." I watched as they held each other and danced slowly, the music a sedate tempo. Scanning the room, I took note of who was here now. There weren't that many of us left, but my eyes nearly bugged out of my head when I spied a familiar face huddled in a corner, blending with the brown upholstery of a booth because he wore all brown and his hair was brown and even his face was now because he'd got a tan. "Volvo Barry," I hissed, hardly believing it.

"What was that?" asked Min, a faraway look in her eyes.

"It's Barry. The guy I kept saying was following me. Look, he's over there. Hiding like a sneak."

Min followed my gaze then said, "He's not hiding. He's just sitting there having a drink. But this is strange. How on earth is he here? I can go along with it being a coincidence him being where you were on the coast, but showing up here is a bit much, isn't it?"

"Yes, it is. He's definitely spying on me. Look at him, being all sneaky." To be fair, he was merely sipping his pint, tapping his foot to the music, and smiling, not taking any notice of anyone. But I still got a tingle at the back of my neck and the hair on my arms was as stiff as Anxious' fur when confronting a polar bear. Not that he ever had.

There was a loud banging at the door and a gruff, angry voice shouted, "Open up, it's the police!"

The room became deathly silent as all eyes turned first to the door, then to Ronnie.

"I wonder if it's about the body?" whispered Min.

"What was that?" asked Harper.

"Nothing." Min mouthed a silent sorry to me and added, "The police are very loud."

"Hey, it's alright everyone. We're allowed to be here," shouted Ronnie, beaming. "Nobody's getting into trouble, not even me. For a change," he laughed. There were nervous giggles but everyone remained quiet as Ronnie swaggered to the door.

"Let me in, or I'll huff and I'll puff," called the policeman.

Ronnie paused, hand to the bolt, and turned with a frown. "Did everyone hear that?"

There were murmurs of agreement and I sank lower in my seat.

"What's wrong?" asked Min.

"You'll see."

Ronnie slid the bolts free, unlocked the doors, and flung them wide.

"About bleeding time," muttered Dad. "Come on, love, it's toasty in here." Dad dragged Mum inside, beamed at Ronnie, and said, "Alright guvnor? Mine's a pint of your finest, please."

"Who are you?" growled Ronnie as Meat appeared beside him, the two men like a solid wall of gangster between Mum and Dad and the cosy interior.

"I'm Jack, this is Jill. We were meant to be here hours ago, but somebody," Dad glared at Mum, "wanted to take the scenic route and sent us into the middle of nowhere. Then we got stuck because of a pot hole and we got a flat tyre, so by the time the repair guy came it..."

Dad trailed off as Ronnie held up a large hand in front of his face and growled, "You said you were the cops. You ain't the cops, are you?"

"Do I look like a copper?" asked Dad, affronted at being interrupted, oblivious to the rest of the room. "That was just my little joke as I guessed there was a lock-in. Saw the light under the door and there was no one in Max's campervan."

Ronnie turned to me and I cringed as he frowned. "You know these two?"

"Yes. Hi, Mum. Hi, Dad."

"Oh, alright, Son."

"Cooee," called Mum. "Hello, Min, love. You doing alright? Did you have a lovely day? I hope my son kept his hands to himself."

"Mum! Of course I did."

"Only because she wouldn't let you touch her, right?" said Dad with a wink and a smile.

If I had a spade, I would have dug a hole and climbed into it.

Min giggled, then waved back and said, "We thought you weren't coming after we heard about the flat tire? It's great you made it."

"Yeah, just peachy," mumbled Ronnie, tutting as he brushed past to secure the door.

"Sorry about that, mate. I didn't mean to cause any bother," said Dad, looking a little sheepish.

"Nah, it's okay. Just got a bit of a surprise there. But welcome, and let me get you a drink. What'll it be?"

While Mum and Dad told him, I whispered to Min, "Why would Ronnie think it strange the police had arrived? He called them. I know they said they might not make it, but if they could they would. What's his game?"

"He probably just panicked that he'd get into trouble. But you're allowed lock-ins as long as you don't charge, and he isn't, so it's all fine."

"Maybe. But he seemed genuinely surprised. Think he has a contact on the local force and they promised not to come? That might explain it."

"Maybe he does." Min turned to check on my parents, and said, "They always make such an effort. Your Mum looks amazing as always."

"She's always been like that. Had her own style. Red dyed hair, the blusher, heavy eye make-up, and the polka dot fifties dresses. It's her thing."

"And the bandana. I like the black and white. It sets off her hair. And your Dad's great, isn't he?"

"He has his moments. He's worn Levi's with fat turn-ups as long as I can remember. Plus a white tee with a leather jacket. He thinks he's John Travolta." Mum and Dad were obsessed with all things fifties, and adored dances, their music, and dressing up. Dad even used to have a pack of cigarettes rolled up in his T-shirt sleeve until he switched to vaping and was distraught that it wouldn't work the same way. After he broke three devices he decided to just give up entirely.

"What are you two whispering about?" asked Dad as they joined us.

"Just saying how lovely you look, Jill," said Min as she scooted over so they had room.

"That's sweet, love. Thank you."

"So, what have we missed? Apart from everything." Dad pointed at Mum just in case we didn't know who he was blaming as he said, "Someone made us go the wrong way and get a flat tire."

"I did not. You took the wrong turn and got us lost. Silly man." Mum winked at Min and said, "They're all the same, aren't they?"

"Max just follows Google Maps," said Min, coming to my defence.

I made the introductions to Stu and Harper, and it was obvious immediately that they'd get on well. Stu and Harper were older by a decade or so, but they had the same sensibilities, were rather alternative like my folks, and once they got on to the topic of music there was no stopping them.

"I think maybe Ronnie killed Dexter," I confided once the others were deep in conversation.

"Stop getting carried away about conspiracies. Not everything is a murder."

"I know that, but I'm sure something's going on. It's just too weird how he acted."

"You said it yourself, they're used to it. And is Meat involved too? He wasn't very emotional either, was he?"

"No, and he might be in on it. I don't know what the set-up is here, but neither were that concerned. Maybe they wanted him out of the picture."

"You need to stop this right now." Min moved in closer after checking nobody was listening to us and said, "Just enjoy the evening. It's been a long day and we're both tired, but there's nothing going on here. If Ronnie did it, he wouldn't have been looking for him earlier."

"Maybe that was his way of appearing innocent."

"Or maybe it's because he is innocent and the poor man in the freezer had a heart attack, or choked, or whatever. Stop looking for trouble."

"You're right! Sorry. I'm starting to think everything is a conspiracy. You can't blame me, though, after the last few weeks."

Min put her hand on my knee and squeezed. "You did brilliantly solving those other horrible deaths, and I'm proud of you. Relax, Max, nothing bad will happen."

I smiled and nodded, my head clearing of fanciful ideas, and decided to just enjoy myself. Yes, it was odd that a man had died how he did, but that's all it was. An unfortunate death.

"So, tell us all about it," said Mum as she drained half her drink.

Min and I exchanged a worried look, but then I understood and asked, "You mean the trip to Portmeirion?"

"Of course, silly. What else would I mean? You haven't been getting into trouble again, have you? Like last time? You can't seem to stay away from bodies. They'll be piling up in the pub next." Mum laughed at her own joke as Dad focused his attention on us.

"What's this about bodies? You been getting into trouble again?"

"Why does everyone assume it's me getting into trouble?" I asked.

"Because you have been," said Mum, her stern look declaring that this was fact and not up for debate.

"Did someone mention bodies?" asked Ronnie as he loomed by the table, hard eyes focused on me.

"I was just telling Max here that he better not be getting into any trouble. Everywhere he goes in that silly van—"

"It's not silly, it's awesome!"

"—he finds bodies. He's very good at discovering who the murderer is, but I keep telling him he needs to stop with his nonsense."

"Mum, I am a grown man and I'm not the one who keeps killing people. But that's not the point anyway.

Ronnie, I was just explaining to Mum that I haven't been up to anything, and was going to tell her about our day at Portmeirion."

"Oh yeah, how did it go? I forgot to ask what with the rush and you getting dragged into helping out in the kitchen."

"He did what?" shouted Dad.

Ronnie frowned and looked from Mum and Dad to me. "Problem?"

"You got Max into the kitchen?" asked Dad.

"Yeah. I, er, couldn't find the chef, and Max stepped in. He's a brilliant cook. Sorry it wasn't very exciting food, Max, but you elevated it to restaurant heights."

"No problem. And, Dad, it was just a few hours. No biggie."

"Are you sure? Are you okay? You haven't got the bug again, have you?"

"No, quite the opposite. It did me good to have a few hours in the kitchen. It made me even more sure that I did the right thing leaving it all behind."

"Then that's okay. I just worry about you, Son. You have a good thing going now," he nodded to Min, "so don't blow it."

"I won't."

"Right, can I get everyone another drink?" asked Ronnie, looking relieved I hadn't told everyone about Dexter.

Everyone gave their order, so Ronnie went to sort them out.

"He's way too intense," noted Dad. "Don't think he liked me pretending to be a copper. Is he a bit dodgy?"

"Just because he looks like a gangster and has a cockney accent, doesn't mean he's dodgy," tutted Mum.

"Doesn't it?" asked Dad, confused.

"No." Mum thought for a moment, then added, "Yes, actually it probably does."

"Don't worry about it, guys," laughed Stu. "Ronnie's an ex-gangster. He turned over a new leaf years ago and now just runs his pub and likes to have the pickle festival."

"How was it?" asked Mum. "I was so looking forward to it, and we missed everything." Dad got another deep scowl for it all obviously being his fault.

"It was utterly bizarre," I admitted. "And Min will explain everything. I want to have a quiet word with Dad and Anxious needs some air. Min, that okay?"

"Um, yes, of course."

I leaned in close to Min and whispered, "I just want to speak to Dad in private. You know why?"

"Yes, but are you sure you should tell him?"

"Positive. I know you think I'm being overly suspicious, but I won't be able to relax unless I tell him. I don't want anything bad to happen."

"Max, nothing bad will happen. But you do what you think is best."

I grabbed Dad and led him through the passage and out of the back door which Ronnie left unlocked for people to use if they wanted to smoke. There was nobody else out here, though, so we moved away from the pub to one of the picnic benches and took a seat.

"Everything okay? Problems with Min? You didn't blow it, did you?"

"Dad, there's no problem with Min. She's here, and that's a good sign."

"Great, because you know we want her back."

"So do I, but that's not what I wanted to talk about."

"I knew it!" he said, smugness radiating from every pore. "You got into trouble again, didn't you?"

"I haven't. Stop saying it like I'm a kid playing with matches."

"You haven't been playing with matches have you? I warned you about that when you were seven."

"Dad, cool it," I laughed, unable to comprehend why he and Mum couldn't accept that I'd grown up. They'd always been like this, and I supposed it was how most parents were. They would always see a little boy, not an adult.

"There's been a death."

"See, this is why we keep telling you to come home."

"And I keep telling you I am home. My van's my home. Listen, let me explain." After I went over what'd happened, and how Ronnie and Meat were so blasé about it and that Ronnie didn't want to phone for help, I asked, "Well?"

"It's right you told me, Son. Us men have to look out for our ladies."

"Oh, so I am a man?" I joked.

"Course. Me and your mum just like to tease you sometimes, but you're a very capable, very smart, and clever guy. I respect what you've done, getting your life together and moving on from your mistakes. That's the true test of a man. And thank you for telling me about this. Whatever this Ronnie character said about keeping quiet, you did the right thing. But relax. By the sounds of it, he did just want to ensure the pub stayed open so everyone could have a good time and he could earn a few extra quid. But he's not taking money for the lock-in, so what difference would it make?" Dad mused, suddenly frowning.

"No, but they did good business after dinner, and he said it would put people off coming. Maybe it's so the barmaid gets a good earner tonight. People are tipping really generously and there's the rescue centre charity that everyone's giving money to. He's a real soppy guy about animals."

"There you go then. Don't read too much into it and let's have a good time."

"Sure, I think you're right. I just wanted you to know in case there are any problems."

"Which there won't be, will there?" came a familiar voice from the darkness.

Chapter 6

"Ronnie, you scared the life out of me!" I snapped, pushing down nerves, annoyed at his scare tactics.

"That's not polite," said Dad, holding Ronnie's stern gaze with an equally hard stare.

"I came out for some air and couldn't help overhearing you."

"Or you came to eavesdrop," said Dad.

"Hey, let's not argue." Ronnie held his hands out to placate us, clearly realising the tough guy act wouldn't work. "Listen, we're men of the world, so let's cut the nonsense. Max, I told you I didn't want the evening disrupted, and that's all there is to this. I'm cut up over Dexter, but what's done is done. Silly sod choked on an onion and it's awful. But if word had gotten out, it would put the punters off and we'd be down on the takings. Plus, and I didn't mention this because I have a reputation to uphold, this evening is more about the charity than anything. The money we make from the festival goes to the rescue centre, and we take a good few hundred with the lock-in. Dexter would have wanted us to carry on."

"So I was right about you wanting to help the charity," crowed Dad, frowning at me.

"Yeah, but people expect me to be the hard man, not some soppy numpty worried about puppies. We understand each other?"

"Sure, Ronnie, I didn't mean to imply anything."

"Hey, I get it. You know a little about my background, that I used to be a bit of a wild one, but that was long ago. I'm a big softy really, but people come here for the vibe, yeah, and they like the tales. Gotta give everyone what they want. So no blabbing."

"Sure, you got it."

"Great, then get yourselves back inside soon. The night is still young, and we have some great games lined up." Ronnie left and we remained silent until the door closed behind him.

"That guy is intense," sighed Dad, pulling out his steel comb and sliding it through his slicked-back hair then patting at the duck's arse to ensure the back was neat.

"He sure is. Think he's on the level?"

"Who knows? But, Max, it's not that unusual to leave a body for a day or so. It happens all the time. People die in their houses, and if it's natural causes the emergency services are often delayed. Or they get the funeral home to collect the body once the police give the all clear. You might find a local copper will arrive at some point in the night and check things out then arrange for the body to be taken tomorrow. Relax. It's all good."

"I think you're right. I'm glad we had this chat. You coming back inside?"

"Course I am. I've got a lot of catching up to do after the day I've had. I need a good few pints to settle my nerves. Your mother is not good with directions."

"Yes, Dad, I'm sure it was all Mum's fault." I winked at him and he laughed. We both knew they were as much to blame as the other.

Back inside, the party was in full swing with the band playing and a few people dancing. Barry was still nursing a drink, but he glanced up when we entered and our eyes met. He smiled and nodded, so I decided to go over and have it out with him once and for all. This had gone on long enough and I wanted to know what on earth he was up to. This time I wouldn't take no for an answer or be fobbed off with some nonsense about it being a coincidence that ever since I started this vanlife he was there at every turn. I might have been paranoid, but only because he was clearly out to get me.

"Barry, this is getting beyond weird. What the hell are you doing here? Why are you so interested in me?"

"Max, can we please not do this again?" sighed Barry as he ran his hands through his lank brown hair. His eyes darted around the room, almost as though he was fearful, then he glanced quickly at me before studying his drink. He was one of those people who never looked you in the eye for long, and it made me feel like he was hiding something. In fact, I was now sure he was.

I sat next to him in the booth, close enough to smell the fish and chips he'd undoubtedly eaten earlier.

"No, I'm not going anywhere until you tell me what's going on."

"Nothing's going on. I keep saying it, but you won't listen. I'm just a guy having a vacation. Initially, it was for a night or two, but I got the bug and decided to take some time off."

"What did you say you did again?"

"Copywriting. You remember. Don't play games."

"Oh yes. But you seriously expect me to believe that? You turn up everywhere I go."

"I was just moving along the coast and you happened to be there. And I'm only here because I heard about the festival."

"You've been here all day? I didn't see you."

"Yes, I was here. People don't notice me. I've got one of those faces, and I know the fact I always wear brown means I'm nigh on invisible to most. It's just the way it is." Barry shrugged like he didn't care, but maybe there was more to it.

"Maybe you don't want to be noticed. Is that it? So you can use your camera?"

"Look, Max, I don't like the way this is going. You make me sound like a peeping Tom. I'm no such thing. I want to enjoy my holiday, that's all. What possible reason would I have for following you?"

"That's what I'm going to find out. Trust me, Barry, I will find out. So why not save us both the bother and come clean?"

"Nothing to tell. Are we done?"

"For now."

Frustrated, and rather freaked out by the guy, I had no choice but to leave Barry with his lies and rejoin the others. Things were heating up, with the party seemingly only just getting going. The band had upped the tempo and were really getting into it, jumping about and encouraging the few remaining people to dance. Never mind that there were only a handful of us in the pub, the atmosphere was buzzing and Mum and Dad had joined a few old-timers jigging about, Dad spinning Mum and the pair of them looking like the professionals they were, having danced every week for their entire lives together.

I made it back to our table and sank into the bench seat beside Min.

"How did it go? You both seemed angry with each other."

"He's up to something and I don't like it. He won't admit to following me, but I know he is."

"Just leave it be. There's no reason why he would be, so steer clear."

"Hey, Max, I just wanted to say you did a great job with the food. Best fish and chips I've ever had," said Stu, beaming.

"Thank you. Glad you enjoyed it."

Mum and Dad joined us, sweating and happy after their dance.

"So much better than that Dexter's cooking," confided Harper with a quick check he wasn't eavesdropping. "I wonder where he got to? Not that Stu minds. He's a weird one."

"How so?"

"Stu and him got into an argument yesterday about his dinner. Dexter made lamb chops, but they weren't cooked right and Stu sent them back. Dexter was fuming and was very rude."

"Drop it, Harper. They don't want to hear about that," mumbled Stu.

"No, he was so rude. He got right up in your face and said you were wrong. I thought you were going to come to blows. And then you were arguing today too. What did he say? We never had a chance to discuss it."

"It was nothing. Just a few cross words. He was still upset I called him out on the food. But it's done."

"You looked really annoyed. What did he say?"

"It was nothing, I told you." Stu folded his arms across his chest and fixed his eyes on the floor, clearly not keen to discuss it.

"This the man who's gone missing?" asked Mum, eyes lighting up at the hint of gossip. "You didn't bump him off, did you, Stu? Maybe he said something so rude you bashed him over the head." Mum cackled, waiting for everyone to join in, but only Harper laughed.

"Yes, maybe you did," agreed Harper, caught up in the moment. "Maybe you cracked him over the head, or force-fed him onions until he exploded."

"Don't be daft," snapped Stu. "That's nonsense!"

"Hey, I was only joking," said Harper, frowning in confusion at Stu's attitude.

Min and I exchanged a look. Why was Stu acting so weird? Did he know something we didn't? Did he have something to do with Dexter's death? Surely not? So what if they had cross words? It didn't mean anything.

"I wonder where that silly man got to?" mused Harper again. "It's very odd to disappear like that."

"Yes, well, let's change the subject," said Stu, then gulped his beer.

"Honey, are you okay? You seem cross. Did I say the wrong thing?" Harper rubbed Stu's arm, eyes drawing him to look at her.

His scowl slowly faded and he smiled warmly at his wife then said, "No, it's fine. I just didn't want to go over a silly argument again. We had a few words, but that was it. It's done with."

"Sure. Now, how about a dance?"

Stu nodded, so they stood, but just then Ronnie took the mike and the band finished their latest tune. All eyes turned to him and conversations stopped as Ronnie cleared his throat.

"Is everyone having a good time?"

A raucous cheer of yes.

"Then let's get to the highlight of the evening. The pickled onion eating competition. All the producers are here."

The group of three pickled onion makers raised a glass to a round of applause.

"We have samples of all their offerings," continued Ronnie as he indicated the neat line of opened jars on the bar. "From traditional, to spicy, to everything in between. The rules are simple. Whoever eats the most onions wins. You go down the line, taking one onion from each jar. There's a pile of forks at the beginning, and you must use a fresh fork for each onion. We don't want any germs being passed around. Health and safety and all that," Ronnie muttered, like it left a bad taste in his mouth. "Who's brave enough to challenge last year's winner, Carter?"

One of the band members, a lanky guy with long brown hair, a rather wild goatee, and twinkling blue eyes stepped forward and took a bow. "I'll wipe the floor with you all," he taunted.

Everyone booed good-naturedly as people began to line up for the competition. The band members joined in, the producers, and even the three men I suspected were gangsters but had apparently turned over a new leaf. Most surprisingly, Volvo Barry also stood and rather shyly took his place in the queue.

Several people left, saying they'd had enough for the night, so Ronnie let them out, leaving just a few of us to indulge in what seemed a very bizarre way to finish off an evening.

"Go on, Son, give it a go," goaded Dad, eyes gleaming with malevolent anticipation.

"No way. My taste buds couldn't handle it. Why don't you try your luck?"

"I do love a pickled onion," he admitted.

Encouraged by the others, Dad dashed over to join the line.

An air of excitement began to build as the competitors eyed up the long line of onions nervously. Those of us not involved cheered on our favourite, all secretly glad we didn't have to devour so many onions, especially the spicy ones near to our side of the pub.

Ronnie cleared his throat again, Meat joined him, and together they counted down.

"Three. Two. One. Go."

Carter was first because he was the reigning champion, and he snatched up a handful of forks, turned and winked at us, then jabbed his first onion expertly, popped it into his mouth, crunched, then swallowed before opening wide to show it was gone.

Everyone clapped as he moved along the line repeating the process, whilst the others began to eat. Carter was closing on the last jar, only three more to go, before he'd have to return to the back and wait his turn. It was survival of the fittest, last man or woman standing, and he showed no signs of slowing.

Jar number twelve now, and things were getting spicy. Carter popped the onion in, put down his fork, and crunched. His eyes watered as he swallowed, and he gasped then bent forward, hands resting on the bar as the room fell silent. But then he coughed, thumped his chest, and declared, "All good," to raucous applause before stepping to his right and confronting the last jar. Jar number thirteen.

Three competitors had already called it a day after just a half dozen or so onions, the spicier jars too much for them to continue, so had stepped back to join Ronnie and Meat while the rest of us joked around. Dad was on jar six and looking a little concerned, but he finished his onion and we applauded as he sidestepped to the next one.

Carter had paused at jar thirteen, with one of the ex-gangsters now beside him who took a tentative bite of his onion, coughed and spluttered, then gasped, "I'm out," and stepped away, face red, eyes watering. Dad moved along until he was next to Carter now, with only half the competitors left.

With a deep breath, Carter jabbed into the jar with his clean fork, held the small onion aloft, gleaming in the light as it dripped heavily spiced vinegar onto the floor, then crunched and began to chew.

The room gasped as Carter's colour rose, a flush that began at his neck and crept up his cheeks until his forehead shone like a beacon.

"So spicy," he groaned as he continued to chew, shuffling away from the row of jars so everyone could move along. Carter staggered to the back of the queue, still chewing, and Dad sidestepped to jar thirteen.

"Unlucky for some," laughed Carter. "But not for me." He opened his mouth to show it was empty, grinning rather manically as he wheezed, the aroma of chilli and vinegar strong in the air.

Everyone clapped. Thirteen onions were done, and Carter was seemingly ready to go again.

"Dad's doing well," I told Mum.

"He does love his onions, the silly sod. His breath will stink for days."

Dad pierced the onion, turned to us, joyous, then held his fork up as he wiggled his eyebrows comically.

He paused as there was a commotion at the beginning of the line.

Carter coughed, and thumped on his chest, but it didn't clear and he stumbled, then reached out to grab the bar. Jars crashed to the floor as he slumped sideways, and Anxious shot up, jumped off the seat, and raced over to snaffle onions as they rained down like giant hailstones.

"Anxious, no! You know they make your stomach funny," I warned, but he either didn't hear, or refused to acknowledge me as he snaffled up onion after onion, not even bothering to chew in his haste to consume as many as possible before he got dragged away.

I jumped up and Anxious darted between Carter's legs, causing him to lose his balance even more. He grabbed hold of a beer pump as he slid along the vinegar-soaked bar, and Ronnie dashed over and helped steady Carter as he regained his footing.

"Are you alright?" gasped Ronnie as Carter straightened, then turned. "Your colour's all wrong. I think you need to rest."

"No, I... I'm fine. Just went down the wrong way. Although, actually, I don't feel so well."

Carter's colour drained, then he began to turn almost green, and his knees buckled.

"Dad, do not eat that onion," I warned as he looked from Carter to me.

"I'll give him a moment," said Dad, lowering the fork.

People crowded around as Carter slumped to the floor, sitting in a pool of onions and vinegar while Anxious took advantage and wolfed a few more before I reached down and hauled him up.

"No more onions. Go and sit with Mum," I told him, holding him at arm's length because his breath absolutely stank.

Anxious whined, eyes drawn to the spilled goodies, but I lowered him and he ran back over to Mum. She made a fuss of him while others righted the knocked jars and Ronnie and Meat helped Carter to stand.

"I'm fine, just very spicy," wheezed Carter.

Everyone sighed with relief, and Carter smirked sheepishly, but then he frowned, and grabbed his throat as his mouth opened and closed but no words came. With Ronnie's help, he was guided to a stool. His strength seemed to have gone and he couldn't remain upright, so Meat held him there and banged on his back, thinking to dislodge a stuck onion.

Carter's eyes rolled up in his head as he gasped, but then his weight became too much and Meat had to lower him to the floor.

Min shouted, "Clear his airways," as she barged through the crowd and sank to her knees then prized his mouth open. She pushed down on his tongue, turned him sideways, and Meat pounded on his back again but Carter was still.

Suddenly, Carter urged, his body animated once more, and he shot to a sitting position, eyes wild. He turned his head, looking at everyone as if not understanding, then he purged a mouthful of onions. He grimaced, then his eyes shut and he keeled over, slammed his head onto the floor, and was still.

They tried everything, but a minute later Min turned to me and said, "He's dead."

Chapter 7

"I'm outta here," said the man who ran a florists.

Ronnie grabbed his arm and stopped him dead in his tracks. "You ain't going nowhere."

"Don't test me, Ronnie," the man growled as his fist clenched and he squared off to the landlord.

"Carter's dead, and it doesn't look like it was an accident to me," said Ronnie.

"What are you on about? He choked on the onions. Silly bugger ate thirteen of them."

"And he's eaten way more than that before. No, this ain't right." Ronnie released the man and turned to the rest of us. "Nobody goes anywhere. Understand?"

There were several shocked murmurs of agreement, but most were quiet, stunned by what had happened, eyes drawn back to poor Carter.

"Dad, do not eat that onion," I warned.

Dad looked from me to the onion still speared on the fork, then released it like the metal was red-hot. The clang of the fork rang out in the quiet room as everyone's attention shifted to the lone jar of pickled onions still standing on the bar in a puddle of vinegar.

I snatched up the offending item and placed it carefully on the bar, not wanting to risk Anxious eating it.

"Is everyone else feeling okay?" I asked. "Dad, you ate the most besides Carter. Are you feeling funny?"

Dad's eyes were slightly unfocused as he stammered, "I... Yes, I'm fine. I think. What just happened?"

"It's bleeding obvious, isn't it?" said Ronnie. "Someone poisoned Carter."

With gasps and a rising tide of emotion and noise, the assembled guests protested or asked how, until Ronnie held up a hand. "If nobody else is ill, then it's got to be jar thirteen. Jack, you're sure you don't feel weird?"

"I do now poor Carter's dead, but I think that's just eating too many onions. I don't feel like I'm going to croak it or anything."

"We need to call the police," screeched one of the three producers, a lady in a dazzling apricot twin-set, dabbing at her eyes.

"Nobody's calling anyone until I get answers. "Pat, that jar belongs to you, doesn't it?" Ronnie pointed at the jar of fiery onions, then fixed his stern gaze on her.

Pat crumpled under the harshness of his stare, tears streaming, but her head snapped up and she parted her curled brown hair and said, "What if it does? Don't you dare suggest I poisoned my own onions. How ridiculous!"

"Carter's dead and it's because of those onions."

"You don't know that. It might have been any of them. Or something else entirely."

"Nobody else has just dropped dead," hissed Ronnie, stepping forward.

"Cool it, Ronnie," said Meat, shifting to intercept. "She's right. Give it a few minutes to see if anyone else feels ill before we jump to conclusions."

"Okay, yeah, good idea." Ronnie turned from Pat and barked, "Everyone sit. This place is locked down from now on until I say otherwise. Anyone dare to call the police and they'll have me to answer to."

"Why can't we call the police?" asked Mum. "That poor man's dead and my Jack might be next."

"Actually, I don't feel so good," Dad complained as he staggered over and slumped onto the bench seat.

"Then I'm calling for an ambulance," I said.

Ronnie marched over as I pulled out my phone and he tried to snatch it from me. I moved away just in time and stood to confront him.

"No phones!"

"Why not?" I demanded. "My dad might die."

"I'm not going to die, am I?" asked Dad in a panic.

"No, because I'm calling for an ambulance." I activated my phone only to find there was no signal. "Has anyone got a signal?"

People checked their phones but nobody did.

"Then it's settled," said Ronnie with a smug smile. "Nobody else is ill, so it can't have been another jar. And no coppers until I know who's going around poisoning people in my goddamn pub!" His fist slammed onto the bar, making the deadly jar of pickled onions bounce. He jumped back and we held our collective breath as the jar wobbled, then sighed with relief as it righted.

"It's not people, it's a person. It's Carter," screeched Pat. "But it wasn't my onions. I sold a lot of jars today and people were sampling them, too, and nobody dropped dead. How dare you!"

"Then it's been tampered with and I want to know who by and why. People are dead."

"Why do you keep saying that?" asked one of the shocked band members. "Carter's dead, but you keep saying people."

"I think you need to tell them," I said, locking eyes on Ronnie and Meat.

"Shut it, Max," ordered Ronnie. "This is my pub and what I say goes. You lot," he jabbed a finger at everyone, "are all suspects. Nobody's going anywhere until I know who did it."

"What's this about?" asked Pat. "Is someone else dead? They are, aren't they?"

"The chef's dead," I said, knowing this had gone far enough. I hadn't been happy about Dexter's death being covered up, but at least Ronnie had called the emergency services. But two bodies, and one looking like it might have been poison, meant they would come as soon as possible.

Murder was much higher on their list of priorities than a natural death.

"I warned you not to tell," said Ronnie, anger bubbling up.

Meat put his hand on Ronnie's shoulder and said, "It's best everyone knows, mate. The cops and ambulance might turn up at any moment anyway, but we need to call them. I'll use the landline."

Ronnie deflated and nodded to Meat who left to use the landline in the back.

Nobody spoke while he was gone, but he returned several seconds later and said, "The line's been cut. No phone, no internet."

"It's a trap!" screamed Mum. "The murderer wants us all dead. It's like those movies where everyone's locked inside a building and they get taken out one at a time."

"Mum, it's okay. Nothing's going to happen," I soothed, indicating to Dad he should look after her. He shifted over and wrapped her in his arms. At least I was now sure he was fine and it must have been the last jar. He was proof of that.

"Why didn't you tell us Dexter was dead?" asked one of the men who ran the bed-and-breakfast.

"I didn't want to ruin the evening and cause a scene."

"What happened to him? Where is he?"

"He's in the freezer. He was dead in the broom closet. Max found him."

"I did, and he had pickled onion all down his apron. Actually, wait here a minute. I need to check on something."

Min tried to stop me, but I smiled at her then raced off.

In the broom closet, I locked eyes on the jar of onions. It looked like Pat's brand, with the same chilli mix inside. Searching around, I discovered a label with Pat's Spicy Ones printed neatly on it tucked away on the shelf, most likely peeled off by Dexter. I left the jar where it was, sure nobody would ever eat one now, then returned to the others.

"Same spicy onions," I confirmed, much to Pat's horror.

"Someone's out to discredit me. They've sabotaged my lovely onions! I'll be ruined!" Pat tumbled backwards to a chair and sobbed, consoled by the two men who made up the healthy competition in the local pickled onion market.

"Nobody's got it in for you, Pat," said Meat. "You make a few dozen jars a year and earn some pocket money, but you aren't exactly a household name."

"Everyone loves my onions," she countered, glaring at Meat. He wilted under the intensity of her stare.

"The question now is, what do we do about this?" asked Ronnie.

"That's obvious, isn't it?" I asked, confused. "We need to go and get help. I'm going out the back, Ronnie, and I'm taking my family with me."

"You ain't going nowhere," he insisted.

"I'll go where I want, when I want. I went along with keeping quiet about Dexter, but only to help you with your business. But you called the emergency services so they'll be here at some point anyway. This is more serious, and if someone's trying to stop us getting in touch with anyone, that's beyond suspicious. Dangerous too. We're not staying."

"Okay, fine. Maybe you do need to go and get help. Because otherwise nobody will come."

"What are you talking about? Of course they will," said Meat. "You called."

"I didn't," admitted Ronnie. "I faked the conversation. There was no signal, which isn't unusual for here, but I never even thought to check the landline."

"You didn't call for an ambulance or the police?" I asked, gobsmacked.

"Nah, but only because I wanted to make sure the night wasn't ruined. It's too important for too many people, and our takings would have been right down. You can't blame a guy for wanting to help save the puppies."

Everyone agreed that you couldn't, and Ronnie had clearly played a winning card by mentioning the rescue centre, but soon suspicion returned to him.

"You covered up a murder?" asked Pat.

"Hey, nobody covered up a murder," protested Meat. "Ronnie, same as me and Max, thought it was an accidental death. Everyone knows what Dexter was like, always sneaking off to stuff his face. We figured he'd just choked, so we put him in the walk-in freezer. But that was pretty dumb, Ronnie," said Meat, shaking his head.

"Yeah, guess it wasn't my best call. Okay, Max, you take your family and go get the cops. Everyone else will stay here."

"How come they get to leave?" asked Pat.

"Because I know Max and Min didn't kill anyone, and his parents only just arrived, so how could they have done it?"

"So you're saying the rest of us are suspects in what? A murder? Poisoning Dexter and Carter?" demanded Pat, hands on hips, daring Ronnie and Meat to agree.

"Well someone did it!" snapped Ronnie.

I shifted to check the others were ready, then turned back to face into the room when Mum's eyes went wide and she gasped.

"Nobody's going anywhere," stated the florist, a hulking man who I was amazed didn't pull a gun from his pocket as he stood and stuffed his hands into his leather jacket.

"Says who?" asked a musician.

"Says me, and says my friends." He nodded to his two acquaintances who, although looking rather bemused, nevertheless stood and joined him.

"You're going to keep us held prisoner even though two men have been killed?" I asked, astonished.

"Nobody's keeping my family held in this death trap," said Dad as he joined me.

"You can try and go, but it won't end well for anyone," said the florist.

"Ronnie, you need to deal with this," I told him. "You lied to me about anyone coming, and now we're being held against our will?"

"He's right, guys," said Ronnie, hands out in a placating gesture. "We can't expect everyone to stay. Someone's up to no good and we can't risk it."

"No, everyone stays," demanded the florist.

"What's your name?" I asked. "In fact, let's get everyone's names. Just so we know who's who."

"I'll do the honours," said Ronnie when nobody offered an introduction. Ronnie used his finger to point everyone out. Starting with himself, then Meat, then Tanya the barmaid, before moving on to me and Min, Mum and Dad, the couple staying in a motorhome, Stu and Harper, then introducing the two living fiddlers, Abe and Gav, before introducing the menacing florist, Harry, and his friends, Monroe and Morris. Last up came Pat and the two other stallholders Jake and Tim.

"What about me?" asked Barry when nobody introduced him.

"Oh yeah, sorry about that. It's Barry, right?"

"Yes."

"And it's about time we found out who the hell you are, Barry," I said, now utterly convinced he was up to something.

"You know this guy?" asked Harry, still in control of the room.

"I do. He's been following me around everywhere I go. Different campsites, always taking photos, and I don't buy that you're just on holiday, Barry. Who are you? Did you have something to do with this?"

"No, I swear I didn't. I'm just a guy taking time off work. This is nothing to do with me and I'm leaving."

Barry stormed forward but Monroe and Morris barred his path and he backed down then resumed his seat.

"I think we need to know more about you, Barry," said Ronnie, shoving past his three old cronies to take back control of his pub and show who was running things.

"I know my rights, and you can't force me to do anything. This has nothing to do with me."

"Is that so?" Ronnie loomed over him and asked, "Then why have you been following Max? He's a good guy, I know that much, and I'm sorry I lied to you, Max," he added, turning.

"I haven't been following you," insisted Barry.

"Let's see who you are," said Ronnie, then he grabbed Barry by the collar, hauled him to his feet, and patted him down. Ronnie came up with a phone and wallet so dropped the phone onto the table and flicked through the wallet. I joined him as Ronnie whistled, his head shooting up to fix Barry with a nasty look.

"That's private. You can't do that!" insisted Barry.

"Private as in private investigator? Because that's what you are, isn't it, Barry Simms? A detective."

Barry slumped back into his chair and people gathered around, curious despite the seriousness of the situation and the dead man on the floor.

"You're a private investigator?" I asked, nonplussed. "You said you were a copywriter. Why lie?"

"Why do you think?" snapped Barry, his whole demeanour changing in the blink an eye.

"That's why I'm asking. I don't understand."

"Because I'm being paid to follow you, of course. Keep an eye on things, see where you went, what you got up to, and report back."

"Why on earth would you do that?" asked Min as she appeared beside me.

"It's my job," shrugged Barry. He seemed taller, and much more confident, and he had no problem retaining eye contact.

"You aren't a very good detective because I kept spotting you. You were always spying on me."

"Yes, well, that was rather unexpected. I've been doing this job a lot of years, and never once have I encountered anyone with such a sixth sense. You pick up on details nobody should, and seem to just have a feel for when things aren't right."

"Is that so?" asked Ronnie with interest. "Tell me more."

"Max here solved a number of murders in recent weeks. Some truly bizarre events that left the police stumped. You heard about the foot found on the beach? How about the campsite murder in Rhyl?"

"That was you?" asked Ronnie. "I knew I'd heard the name before. Max Effort, of course! Well, it seems we're in luck, everyone." Ronnie beamed at the room of utterly dumbfounded people. "Don't you get it? Max is going to figure this out."

"Now wait just a minute. I don't think this is the same thing at all."

"Course it is, love," shouted Mum. "You can do it. Figure it out."

"Yes, go on, Son. Who did it? Who's the killer?"

"This isn't a game! Two people are dead, most likely poisoned, someone's cut the phone line, there's no mobile signal, and this guy's been following me for weeks."

"Is that it?" asked Mum. "Has he solved it already? Was it Barry?" she asked Dad, confused.

"No, love, Barry's just a pervert who likes spying on chefs. I bet he stole Max's underwear too. That's what they all do."

"I am not a pervert! And I did not steal his underwear! I was doing my job. But, Max, you are annoyingly good at figuring things out. I was stumped by the crimes, same as the police, even though I was following you everywhere. Most times you never spotted me, but you did more often than I'd have liked."

"I'm still not getting this," I admitted. "Why were you following me at all? And do not," I warned, "say it was because you were paid. I'll throttle you if you do."

"Fine. The truth is..." Barry's words were cut off as he began to cough, his eyes widening in fear, worried he'd been poisoned.

I started coughing, too, my eyes watering, and soon everyone in the room was doing the same thing. Something vile, and utterly noxious, was caught in the back of my throat and I feared for everyone's lives as the smell intensified and a deadly gas filled the air.

"What... what is that?" gasped Ronnie as he shoved past Barry to get as close to the door as possible.

"Are we under attack?" shouted Tanya from behind the bar where she'd retreated.

"Help us. It's coming from over here," wailed Mum as Dad grabbed her and they raced through the exit to the corridor that led to the kitchen, the bathrooms, and more importantly, the back door. Had Ronnie even locked it yet?

"What is it?" coughed Meat as he slapped a hand over his mouth, his eyes red and streaming. "I can hardly breathe."

"I'll open the doors. We need to get out." Ronnie unlocked the double doors with shaking hands, then threw the bolts clear and flung them open. Fresh air rushed in to weaken the gas as everyone clamoured for freedom.

"Mum, Dad, we're going out the front," I shouted, but I assumed they had already left.

Anxious took this moment to jump from the bench seat and dash between the legs of everyone, making a break for it.

"I think I know who was gassing us," I chuckled, my eyes shining.

"I'd recognise that smell anywhere," Min giggled nervously.

"Yeah, Anxious ate too many pickled onions and his stomach can't handle it. He gets gassy."

"Very gassy. Remember when he did it in the bedroom and we thought we might be getting poisoned by a gas leak from the mains?"

"I do," I laughed. "We had the inspector out at three in the morning and nobody could find the source until we found Anxious in the kitchen on the counter eating more onions we'd forgot to put back in the fridge. It cost a fortune."

"He does like a pickled onion."

"If I never seen one again in my life, it will still be too soon. What are we going to do, Min?"

"We're going to go and get some fresh air, then we'll call the police."

"Who could have done such a thing? Who do you think it was?"

"I couldn't even hazard a guess at this point. Half of them are dodgy gangsters, the rest have something to hide, I'm sure. Stu argued with Dexter about something, the picklers are weird, and I wouldn't trust Ronnie as far as I could throw him."

"But it's not Ronnie, is it?"

"He faked calling for an ambulance and reporting Dexter's death, then he was going to lock us in. And then his buddies threatened everyone."

"Yes, but only to find out who did it."

"Or to cover their own tracks and kill the rest of us. Someone cut the phone line, and nobody has a phone signal. It's been planned, and that doesn't feel safe at all."

"Then let's go and get the police."

"I agree. They can sort this mess out."

"I'll grab some water." I skirted around the bar, careful not to slip on the vinegar and onions. It felt strange being on the other side, but I fished around for bottles of water, reaching low to the back of the open shelves. I knocked several over and found a small box there, a light blinking.

"What's wrong?"

"Do you know what this is?" I asked Min as I held up the small black box.

"No. What is it?"

"It's a signal jammer. It negates a mobile mast's signals. This is why we couldn't make any calls."

Min and I exchanged a nervous glance then looked out of the door.

"So the killer must be one of them?" she asked.

"Looks that way."

"Max, I am never going to eat another pickled onion in my life."

"And I'm never going to the pub again." Min cocked her head and waited. It didn't take long. "Okay, forget I said that. But I'm staying in the beer garden when I do fancy a pint."

Chapter 8

We found everyone easily enough thanks to the bickering and Ronnie's repeated shouts for calm. We followed the noise around to the beer garden, lit up with the security lights.

After explaining about the source of the gas, I asked Barry, "Do you know what this is?" as I held up the signal jammer.

"Of course. But how do you know?"

"Saw it in a movie, I think. Or a show."

"Let me see that." Harry, the overbearing florist, snatched it from my hands and grunted. "So somebody definitely wanted everyone to stay away from the cops."

"What is it? Let me see," said Mum, brushing past the others with her new bestie, Harper, by her side.

"It's just a little metal box," she said, disappointed.

"It's for jamming phone signals. It's why nobody can use their phones," I explained.

"This is ridiculous. I bet it was Ronnie all along. Where did you find it?"

"Behind the bar, hidden with the water bottles. I got some, if anyone wants a drink." I dropped several water bottles onto a picnic bench and people snatched them up, Dad being one of the first. Just as he was about to take a drink, I said, "Um, actually, maybe this isn't such a sensible idea. After the onions being poisoned."

Dad froze with the bottle to his lips, then nodded and returned it to the table. "Good point."

"Smash the damn thing," said Monroe, and grabbed it from Harry who snarled but let the man keep it. He threw it to the ground then stomped with his boot and the thing crunched; the light flickered then died.

"Check your phones," said Mum.

Everyone dutifully pulled out their phones and checked. Sure enough, there was a signal.

"Don't everyone try to call at once. It will get messy," said Ronnie, back in command. "Max, you do it."

"Okay, if you're sure?"

Everyone agreed I should make the call, so I did. When I hung up, I realised they had crowded in close and were waiting for me to say something.

"Well?" asked Dad.

"They said don't touch anything, stay out of the pub, nobody is to leave, and we should try to remain safe."

"How do we do that if one of us is the killer?" asked Harper, stepping away from the others with Stu and studying everyone warily. "Or it might be someone who left before the competition started."

"It could have been anyone at any point during the day," said Pat.

"I guess we need to split into groups of people we know and trust, or maybe we should sit separate and everyone keeps an eye on everyone else," I suggested.

"I'm not sitting without you and Min and Jack," declared Mum, affronted.

"No, of course not. Then we'll sit together as it definitely wasn't any of us. Everyone else needs to decide for themselves. But nobody can leave. The police want to talk to all of us."

"And when will that be?" asked Morris, who had been very quiet until now. He looked just like his partner, Monroe. Slim, with a smart beard, nice tan, brown eyes, in simple jeans and a dark linen shirt. Both were affable and friendly, but there was no mistaking the underlying gangster vibe, especially now the stress levels were heightened.

I shrugged. "They said as soon as possible, but I don't know."

"Then they can come and talk to us at home," said Morris.

"Agreed," said Monroe. "We have guests, and we can't leave the house unattended. We should have been home already. It's awful about Carter, but we have our own livelihood to consider."

"You better have a re-think about that," said Ronnie.

"Or what, Ronnie? You aren't the boss any longer, and you don't get to call the shots."

"Is that right?" he spat, stepping forward with Meat by his side.

"Yeah, so back off."

"You got it all wrong," said Ronnie. "I wasn't giving you an order, although it's good to know what you really think, guys. I was trying to protect your business. What, you'd rather the police come banging on the door at all hours, waking up your guests, would you? Lights flashing, asking questions about murders? They won't know a thing about it unless you go home now and they get woken up."

Morris and Monroe exchanged a look, then nodded.

"You're right. Yeah, smart call. And I didn't mean that. I was just getting worked up. You're still the man, Ronnie,"

"Don't you forget it," he grumbled, but shook Morris' hand when it was offered.

We settled into an awkward silence in groups at the picnic tables or standing where everyone could be seen. Anxious kept whining, and I understood why, so told Min I'd take him for a walk and had plenty of poo bags. She said she'd come with me, so we rose and I called for Anxious. He farted his way over and gratefully followed us around to the front then towards the trees.

He shot off, but his white and brown-spotted fur was lit up by the lights so it was easy to keep an eye on him.

"Are you okay?" I asked Min. "This is quite intense."

"It's terrifying. How are you staying so calm?"

"I didn't realise I was. I'm shaken up too. Sorry I didn't tell you about the other guy, Dexter."

"I understand. You didn't want to scare me, and you didn't know anything untoward had happened."

"No, but it still felt wrong. I should have followed my instincts. It didn't feel right, and now I know why."

"Who could have done such a thing, Max? And why? Why here? Why when everyone was locked in like that? It's a big risk when we were all there together."

"That's a lot of questions I don't have the answers to."

"Why would they kill the chef? And that poor fiddler? I suppose the same person did it."

"It was two jars of the same onions, so I'm guessing so. Assuming they poisoned a few jars. Maybe they left one out for Dexter knowing he was into them, and they would have known Carter would eat the onions first as he won last year."

"Which means it was someone who was here last year?"

"Yes, but they all were apart from us. Everyone else is a regular."

"Except for Barry," Min reminded me.

"Yes, except him. What's that all about? Why is he being paid to follow me? I need to speak to him."

"And you will, but this is more important at the moment. What are we going to do?"

"We wait for the police, then we answer their questions and hope they can figure this thing out."

"And how likely is that?"

"I honestly don't know. Maybe they can trace the poison, test people's fingers or something to see if they came into contact with it. This is beyond me."

"You'll figure it out."

"You think?"

"You have every other time. I believe in you." Min beamed at me, then stood on tiptoe and planted a warm kiss on my cheek. "I did have a lovely day until people started dropping like flies. Who would have thought there'd be poison and pickles at the pub?"

"Not me."

Once I'd cleaned up after Anxious, who seemed mighty relieved and smelled a lot better, too, I decided to sneak back into the pub so explained to Min and she agreed to come with me. Mum and Dad were safe, as no way would anyone try anything with so many pairs of eyes on everyone.

We went in through the front door, the smell of vinegar incredibly strong inside, even overpowering the beer and what lingered of Anxious' noxious emanations.

"What are we looking for?" asked Min.

"I have no idea. Anything that doesn't seem right. Maybe we need to check everyone's vehicles, but that's way beyond us and they'll be locked up anyway."

"And definitely overstepping the line. Let's be sure not to touch anything. We don't want to get poisoned ourselves."

"You're right. I better hold on to Anxious just in case." I explained to the little guy what I was about to do, and he wagged happily, never minding being cuddled as he could catch up on some face licking.

I regretted it instantly, as his breath absolutely stank and he was beyond excited to be up so late with so many pickled onions everywhere. He seemed to think I was going to hand them over, but he was sorely disappointed. Min and I spent a while searching the pub, but there was nothing to be seen apart from poor Carter who I tried to avoid studying too hard.

Everyone had taken their belongings with them, so there weren't even coats or bags to check, and none of the storage rooms or the kitchen offered up anything.

At a loss, we returned outside and just in time, too, as police cars and an ambulance arrived with lights flashing, sirens whoop-whooping, lighting up the clientele and the pub in blue and red, making them look like Smurfs or demons.

Anxious stayed close to us as we joined Mum and Dad, both subdued. It was late now, gone midnight, and everyone was clearly feeling it. As the reality of this settled in, people were weary and wanted to go home to bed. That was not going to happen.

Ronnie went to greet the first officers to arrive, and explained what had happened. We were then swarmed by a veritable army of police officers, all trying to secure the scene whilst ensuring everyone remained safe and we were kept apart.

It took quite a while for things to settle down and then detectives arrived, followed by photographers, and a whole horde of specialists, although we were kept away and were busy talking to officers, so it was hard to keep track of exactly what was going on.

My family remained together and we explained everything that had happened to an affable constable, but then when a detective came to speak with us we had to go through the entire thing again. After hours, I was taken aside by the lead detective and asked to explain things yet again, this time without any interruption from Mum and Dad, which did mean it went more smoothly. I described events in the kitchen, about finding the body, Ronnie and Meat wanting to put him in the freezer, and even about Ronnie saying he had called when he hadn't.

The detective confirmed that Ronnie had already admitted as much, then went on to say that she knew who I was, had heard about me from friends on the force, and had even called Julia and Malc from Rhyl to get up-to-speed on me. She said I wasn't a suspect, but that I should remain here so they could speak to me again in the morning.

I wasn't too happy about that, and said so. If people were being murdered, shouldn't we go somewhere else? Somewhere safer?

DC O'Connell didn't agree, reminding me that as long as the van was locked we would be safe, and that we would be needed for questioning in the morning and possibly to come to the police station. I said I'd be happy to do that, but no way was I staying at the scene.

But in the end I acquiesced because she reminded me of one other very important point. This was currently the safest place in the area as there was a whole team of people here and they would remain until daybreak and beyond going over things and trying to uncover what had really happened. Everyone was allowed to return to their homes, but for some of us that meant simply sleeping in our campervans, or in Barry's case, his tent, which was tucked into a corner of the allocated field for sleeping overnight.

The three ex-gangsters, and the two remaining band members, were all allowed to leave, but the band members, Abe and Gav, said they would stay in their tour van as they'd had a few drinks, even though they only lived locally. The stallholders had campervans, and remained, even though they too lived in the nearby village of Boar.

Beyond weary, and utterly dazed by the whole thing, it was almost three in the morning when I unlocked the campervan with Min, Mum, Dad, and Anxious all huddled close. Everyone was so tired that we just collapsed onto the bed in a heap, squashed like sardines. It was obvious straight away that it wasn't going to work, so I left them to it and quietly crept outside with Anxious who curled up at my feet as I settled into the camping chair and watched the police come and go.

I must have dozed off at some point, as I woke to daylight and an endless procession of police and associated specialists. I spied DC O'Connell so eased myself up, my back stiff from the chair, and left Anxious snoring as I padded across the dewy grass to where she was sitting on a picnic bench with her hands wrapped around a cup of coffee.

"Any more of that going around?" I asked, my throat parched.

"Over there. Just don't get your hopes up. Police coffee is renowned for being the worst."

"No fancy coffee machine or a deal with Starbucks?" I asked.

"As if. But it isn't so bad really. And it's hot and wet, so what can you do?"

I got myself a drink then returned and sat on the opposite side of the bench. The coffee wasn't awful, but it certainly wasn't great either.

"That was good of you to keep guard like that outside," noted DC O'Connell.

"Thanks, but it was only because there was no room in the camper and Dad snores terribly."

"Call me Dolores, by the way. No need to be formal like earlier."

"That's a pretty name."

"My Mum adored The Cranberries, so yes, that means I'm no ancient DI but a young DC with plenty to prove. So don't do anything that will make me suspect you, Max."

"Wouldn't dream of it." I'd placed her at my age, but she must have been a little younger than me, with a solid figure, a no-nonsense attitude, and a very odd style of dress. She wore a faded denim shirt, matching jeans with a large buckle at her belt, and cowboy boots. Not usual for a detective, but I hadn't met that many.

"Anything you can tell me? If you spoke to Julia, you know I'm to be trusted, and might be able to help."

"Max, what is with you?" Dolores lowered her coffee and fixed her best detective stare on me.

"How'd you mean?"

"I mean, how does one man keep encountering murders like this? It's a bit freaky. Aren't you concerned?"

"I was when it happened for the second time, but now that it's happened again, I'm not. I know that's counterintuitive, but it confirms what I thought the last time there was a murder. This is why I'm living this vanlife. It's as though I've been chosen. A calling. I know that sounds like nonsense, but it truly feels like this is why I'm travelling around. Helping to solve these terrible cases."

"It doesn't sound silly at all. That's why I became a cop. To help solve crime. It's my calling. It feels like the right thing to do."

"There you go then. I never expected any of this, but I'm pretty good at catching the little details, and I might be able to help figure this out."

"Maybe you can. We'll see."

"What I'm getting at is you can trust me. If there's anything you discovered, then I'd like to hear about it. I don't mean break any rules, divulge information you'd get into trouble for sharing, but just know that anything you do tell me is in the strictest confidence and I swear I'll never tell."

"That's good to hear, and I would tell you what I could. But here's the thing, Max. I have nothing to share. You already know as much as the rest of us. We're at a dead end right now, but it's very early days. Just to recap, here is what we've learned. Dexter the chef was poisoned, the coroner's office confirmed that from a preliminary test, but he's been taken away just like Carter to be checked thoroughly. But yes, both poisoned by the spicy pickled onions."

"That seemed most likely."

"And someone cut the phone lines and used a signal jammer so nobody could make any calls."

"I don't get why at all. Any ideas?"

"No. It seems pointless to me, but who knows what was planned next?"

"Anything else?"

"The rest of the onions have been taken for testing, but the ones out on the bar were clean as nobody else is ill. That will be a relief for everyone, I'm sure."

"It will. Dad was freaking out about it and we were worried."

"And now to the juicy bit."

"Yes?" I leaned forward, eager to hear.

"They're a bunch of ex-cons and gangsters. Nearly all of them are dodgy."

"Oh," I sighed, deflated. "Yes, I already knew that."

"Did you?" Dolores frowned, then asked, "About all of them?"

"About Ronnie, Meat, Harry, Monroe, and Morris. Dexter was a gangster, too, wasn't he?"

"Yes, they all were. Part of a gang from back in the day down south. Crooks, but pretty small-scale actually, and they all served a little time but nothing too serious. Their bark is definitely worse than their bite, if you get my drift. They all play on it, but they weren't that much of a problem even back in the day."

"Oh, okay. I assumed they were big-time gang members or had done some serious stuff."

"Not really. But Stu and Harper, that's a different story entirely."

Chapter 9

My eyebrows made a break for the top of my head as I said, "Do tell. They just seem like a pair of ageing rockers."

"And they are, to some extent. Both were roadies for several heavy metal bands many years ago, and that's where they met. I'm talking forty years ago. Good kids, no issues, but once they hooked up it seems they became quite notorious. I spoke to a retired detective who remembered them well. His name was on their files. They got involved in several serious cases of fraud and he believed quite a lot else, and they served five years each."

"Wow. They don't seem the type."

"Trust me, they often don't. I'm not saying they had anything to do with this, but it's more of a heads-up. Keep an eye on them. There's nothing violent in their past, but with ex-gangsters and musicians being poisoned, there's no denying there might be a connection. So tread carefully and do not let my boss or any of the other detectives get wind of you snooping. I'm only telling you this because by all accounts you're going to get involved no matter what you're told, so be careful."

"I will. And thank you, Dolores. I really appreciate this. What happens now?"

"Now we try to figure out this mess. We're about done here. Everything has been checked, double-checked, photographed, tested, fingerprinted, and as far as that goes it's a dead end. Too many people touched the jars in the pub and the one in the broom closet was totally clean apart from Dexter's prints. It could have been anyone. We have no clear motive, a worryingly long list of suspects, and we can't keep everyone here indefinitely."

"This is a tricky one."

"What I need," she said, leaning forward and lowering her voice, "is an ear to the ground. I bet Stu and Harper will want to leave today, same for the remaining band members, and the stallholders, too, so anything you can glean from them will be immensely useful. Having everyone in one place makes our job easier, but half of them will most likely be gone in a few hours. I know I would."

"What about Pat? They are her onions."

"She's a handful," sighed Dolores, smiling weakly. "Very feisty and indignant. Her stock has been confiscated, for obvious reasons, and is being tested, so it won't be returned any time soon. Same for the others. We can't take that risk. Even the food from the pub is strictly off limits. Ronnie's not happy, but until this is cleared up we can't allow him to open again."

"How did they poison the onions? What was it?"

"We don't know. We just can't say, and that means a major headache for everyone involved. We're up to our necks with this one as jars of pickled onions being laced with poison is a total disaster. We have no idea who came here, no idea how many jars were sold as the vendors weren't exactly great at keeping records, although we have a rough idea, and although we assume the victims were targeted on purpose, we can't say that with a hundred percent conviction."

"You mean there could be more poisoned jars out there somewhere?" I asked, aghast.

"Maybe. It's doubtful. These victims were chosen as far as I'm concerned, but there's no guarantee."

"So any number of people might have died last night from poisoning? Or years from now when they crack open the jar?"

"It's possible," admitted Dolores. "Which is why I want you to snoop. Got it?" Dolores drained her coffee and stood. "It was nice meeting you, Max."

"You too. Thanks for confiding in me. I'll do my best."

"I know you will. We all will. It will be quiet around here today as we're done, but if anyone gets ill call for an ambulance immediately."

"Of course. Dolores, do you really think more people are at risk?"

"No. This was premeditated and beyond cruel. It was aimed at the two deceased. We're sure of that. Plenty of others ate Pat's spicy onions yesterday and nothing bad happened to any of them while they were here. We've managed to trace a few people that Pat and the others knew from the area and everyone is fine, but we can't rule anything out."

"Okay, that's a relief. Kind of."

"Yes. Here's my card. Call me if you hear anything, or think of something we might have missed. I won't say we're relying on you, Max, but we are relying on you." Dolores winked, then gave me a cheeky smile.

"So no pressure then?" I laughed.

"Of course not. And I'm only pulling your leg. This isn't your job, but it is mine, so I'd be remiss if I didn't pursue every avenue. Understand? You're another set of eyes right in the heart of this, and people say things to civilians they would never say to the police." With a nod, Dolores went to join a group of detectives and officers who were seemingly ready to leave.

I watched them pack up while I finished my coffee, and ten minutes later nothing remained of the chaos apart from spent coffee cups, more crime scene tape than could have possibly been necessary, and a very sad-looking Ronnie, who eased under the tape at the front door to his pub then just stood there, looking bedraggled and utterly distraught.

What exactly had we got involved in here? How had the onions even been poisoned? I didn't know of anything that could act so rapidly, not that I knew much about poison. It was a real concern that there could be countless people out there with what amounted to a jar of poison in their kitchen, but would the killer go that far? Dolores didn't seem to think so, and I agreed, but nothing was certain. I guess the fact that nobody else had reported a mysterious death or any of the other customers had become ill yesterday was enough to assuage fears, but whoever did this was clearly unhinged, so they had to be found.

"How are you doing, Ronnie?"

"About as good as I look," he grumbled, rubbing at his face as though he was one step away from reality and wanted to wake himself up. "Damn, my beard's grown and I didn't shave. Maybe I should grow it out like you?"

"It's always an option. Saves on razor cuts."

"You're up early. Couldn't sleep either?"

"Not really. It was cramped in the camper so I slept outside, but the police woke me."

"Yeah, me too. I was just nodding off and then they were banging about inside. Damn place is in utter chaos. They took so much stuff too. All the food. Said it was too dodgy because of Dexter being in the freezer, and anything fresh is gone too. They bagged the lot and took it away. And they shut me down, Max. This is my livelihood."

"Insurance will cover it. Get on it straight away and put in a claim."

"Yeah, I will, but it isn't the same. And what about my reputation? This might ruin me. Ruin me and Meat. And poor Dexter. Nobody deserves to die in a broom closet eating a sneaky jar of bloody picked onions. It's undignified."

"He went out doing what loved. Try to look at it like that."

"Yeah, maybe."

"What did the police tell you? What's next?"

"They're going to inform next of kin, perform autopsies, try to discover what poison was used, and I can't open until I get the all clear from them. What an utter mess."

"I'm so sorry. It was a fun night, too, until it wasn't."

"It was, wasn't it?" he said, brightening. "But now it's ruined. I suppose you'll be off first thing?"

"No, I'll stick around for a while if that's okay? I'm guessing my folks will leave early, and I expect Min will want to go, too, but Anxious and I will be here to help out if you need us. As long as it's alright to keep the campervan here? I know it's only meant to be for a night or two."

"Max, stay as long as you want. There won't exactly be a queue of people wanting to visit here now, and if you're serious, then I'd appreciate it anyway. After what I heard about your recent exploits, you're just the guy I need to help figure this out. We need to find who did it and we got to do it quick-smart. I don't like guys getting whacked on my watch. Under my roof!" Ronnie slammed his fist into his palm, face twisted in anger, then his shoulders slumped and he turned back to me. "Sorry. It's just so frustrating and so damn sad. They were good guys."

"I know, and we'll do our best to solve this. What do you think happened? I mean, apart from the obvious? Do you trust your friends? The old buddies from back in the day?" I was trying to tread carefully, but I had to ask.

"Those guys? Look, Max, I know we come across as big London gangster types, but we were strictly small-fry, and not as nasty as you might think. Punters like a bit of drama and enjoy coming somewhere slightly dodgy, you get me? Even the guys at the bed-and-breakfast play on it, and so does Harry at the florists. If you have a reputation it draws in the business. The old dears love it, the yummy mummys, too, and the guys eat it up. But we're nice blokes really. And do I trust them? Not a bloody chance. They're as bent as a coat hanger, but they're friends and one thing they ain't is killers. I've known them a long time, same as Meat, and not one of us has ever killed a guy."

"Okay, I understand. And what about everyone else? How well do you know them?"

"A little, not a lot. I know Tanya the best. She's been working behind the bar for a few years now and although she looks like one scary lady, she's an angel. She lives here, you know? Part of the family. She lost her parents a few years back and apart from her grandfather we're her only family. Not through blood, but in every other way that matters."

"Oh, I didn't realise. How come she lives here?"

"Because rent costs a fortune." Ronnie looked at me like I was suddenly a stranger. "Max, you have money, right?"

"Some. I used to earn plenty and made a few property investments. It means I can live off the rental income. It's not a great deal of money, but it means I don't have to work for a living. I sold a small house recently, but that's money that went towards the VW and the rest is there for if I ever buy another place. The main house I left to Min when things went sour."

"I get it. You aren't loaded, but you're still a little removed from what it's like out here for most people. Times are hard, rents and mortgages are stupid expensive, and young uns like Tanya can't afford anything but a crappy flat in a dodgy area."

"So she stays here as part of her wages?"

"No, rent free. I pay her the regulation wage, and she chips in with bits and pieces to cover her rent. She sorts out her own food or gets something from the kitchens, but I do right by her. I'm lucky like you. I have a little money, but I still need this place up and running to keep Tanya in a job, the new chef, whoever that will be, and there's the cleaning lady, and the suppliers for booze and food. It's all local, and we do right by them. You get me?"

"I get you."

"So, fancy a job? You were awesome yesterday and the punters loved the grub. You'd fit right in. I can even offer free board and lodging." Ronnie grinned, knowing I'd say no.

"That's a hard pass from me," I laughed. "But thanks for the offer."

"Can't blame a guy for trying. Come inside for a moment."

"What for?"

"Just in case inspiration hits. You never know." Ronnie ducked under the tape and entered his pub.

With a shrug, I followed him in, the familiar tang of beer and vinegar still strong, but combined with other, more recent chemical smells, presumably used by the teams testing for various substances.

"Look at this place. What a mess. The cops don't clean up anything. You have to leave it exactly how it was until they're finished. I told the cleaning lady to take the day off as there's glass and chemicals and all sorts and I don't want to risk anything, so I'll get it sorted myself."

"I'll give you a hand."

"No, leave it to me and Tanya. Meat will be up later. He can help too. You spend time with your family and that lovely wife of yours."

"Ex-wife," I reminded him.

"Yes, but I can tell you guys love each other. Bide your time, Max, and win her back."

"I will."

"So, what do you make of this? The coppers tested for fingerprints and we all had ours taken, right? Look at this powder they left. And I can't believe they took the food."

"They're just being cautious, Ronnie."

"I know, but it's a major headache. Poor Dexter, poor Carter. What poison even does that?"

"I have no idea. It worked fast, that's for sure."

"Really fast. I thought poisons usually took hours to work, or if they happened that quick it wouldn't kill you right away. It's beyond freaky."

"What I don't get is why jam the phone signal? What difference did that make?"

"Beats me? Guess they didn't want anyone calling the police too soon after."

"Yes, but you could have called after we found Dexter. Or I could have."

"Sorry about that. I was worried about business, but should have put him first. If I had, Carter would still be alive."

"Don't beat yourself up over that. How were we to know?"

"True, but it still happened. The signal jammer is a real mystery. Whoever did this must have had their reasons though."

"Yes, but what? It's nonsensical. Anyone could have just left and driven to get help, and what did they gain by stopping anyone from calling anyway?"

"My guess is they planned something else. Or maybe they wanted the delay for some reason like maybe the poison to definitely work."

"Could be. Or..."

"What? Come on, you obviously thought of something."

"What if the jammer was so no calls were received?"

"So nobody here got interrupted?"

"Could be. If Carter got a call he might have not been first in the line. Or maybe the killer didn't want any interruptions from anyone, just in case it ruined their plans."

"I like the way you think, Max. You come up with stuff I never would, so keep that brain of yours going and see what else you can figure out. I'm gonna get started on cleaning up. The police said it was okay now. Have a nose around and see if there's anything else that sparks an idea."

While Ronnie began clearing things away, I did the rounds of the pub again, this time going slowly and inspecting everything.

Trying to get into the head of a killer was impossible for me to do, but I tried to at least think what they might have been doing to have pulled this off. When did they poison the onions? How did they ensure the right jar was used? Why didn't they want any calls coming in or going out? And what was the point anyway? Why kill two men in the first place?

I found nothing under the seats, stuffed down the sides, or stuck under tables. There was nothing behind the bar, nothing in cupboards or drawers, and I came up with zero clues after a fruitless search.

Ronnie was busy sweeping the floor when I finished, so I asked, "Who picked the jars of onions for the eating competition? I know it was split roughly between the three producers, but did they just hand the jars to you, or did you select them?"

"They handed them over. They gave me them in the afternoon so we'd be sure we had enough. They sell fast, so we always do that."

"So Pat gave you the jar of spicy ones herself?"

"Yes, she did. But it couldn't be her, could it?"

"It's pretty obvious if it was. You wouldn't be that blatant about killing someone. Where did you keep them once they were brought in?"

"Just behind the bar on the shelf."

"And who had access to them?"

"Me, Meat, and Tanya."

"That's it?"

"Yeah, that's it," he said, face sour. "Max, the police already went over this. No way Meat or Tanya did it, and I know I'm innocent. I ain't a killer."

"Of course not. But someone is. What's the deal with Meat? He a partner in this place?"

"Not really. I own it. It's my gaff. He never was good with his cash, and when I moved up here he was in a bit of bother so decided to tag along. I invited him. We're best buddies. He gets a wage for being like a joint landlord. Understand, Max, I look after my own. Meat's a great guy, but he ain't the smartest. He's had one too many knocks to the head over the years. He used to be a fighter. I look after my own," he repeated, fixing me with a hard stare. "Don't go accusing him of anything. He's a good guy. I look out for him, and he looks out for me and helps around here. We're a team."

"Sure, Ronnie. I didn't mean to be insulting."

"Nah, you weren't. I asked you to help and you are. But understand one thing. Meat didn't do it, neither did Tanya."

"So who else could have got to the onions?"

"I guess someone could have come in and switched jars easily enough. Or put the poison in when nobody was behind the bar. We were outside a lot for the festival."

"Or it might have been poisoned before it was brought in."

"Yeah, course. That's most likely it. Someone put it in the jar, Pat had no idea, and the rest is history."

"Okay, I'll see you later."

"Later, Max, and watch your back, yeah?"

"You can count on it."

Chapter 10

It was still incredibly early and nobody else was up yet, or if they were, they were keeping a low profile. I didn't blame them. The sense of fear was palpable in the early morning, misty air, but already the temperature was rising with the sun and it would be another scorcher of a day.

Anxious was where I'd left him, but his nose twitched as I approached silently, and then a lazy eye opened. I patted my thighs to beckon him over without disturbing anyone, so he stretched out, yawned, then skipped over, tail wagging, and rubbed against my legs until I bent and stroked his head.

"Every single morning without fail," I laughed, always amazed how excited he was to see me after just a few hours.

Anxious whined, asking for a walk, his ears primed for rabbits.

"I don't think there are any rabbits around here, but we can always go and look. Now's a good time."

Anxious yipped in agreement, so we headed off towards the river then followed its course upstream, weaving through the trees. The only reason I didn't mind Anxious chasing the rabbits was because he saw it strictly as fun. He had never tried to kill them, and the one time a daring buck had stood its ground he hightailed it with his tail between his legs and returned to me in utter confusion. He was playing, and would never hurt them.

Ten minutes into our peaceful walk—which was exactly what I'd needed to clear my head—Anxious came racing back to me, then skidded to a halt, hackles raised, tail straight.

"What is it, boy? Did you see a big, scary rabbit?" I teased, picturing the scene.

Anxious whined, then did an about-turn and growled, low and menacing.

"Okay, let's go check it out. But quietly. No making a noise, and no running off. Remember, it's dangerous at the moment, and we need to be mindful of that."

Anxious either understood the words or the tone, so kept pace beside me as I slowly and silently weaved between the trees, using them as cover. It didn't take long before voices drifted my way on a subtle breeze, so I slowed until I figured out the direction, then hurried from tree to tree, watching for twigs in the long grass.

The voices rose in volume so I put my back to a tree and waited a moment, then peeked out, homing in on the conversation.

Stu and Harper were in a clearing, standing apart, both rigid, angry scowls on their faces.

"...to know exactly what you did." Harper put her hands on her hips, glaring at Stu.

"Are you mad? I'm not about to admit to murder! We both know we've done bad things in the past, but that was long ago."

"So what was the argument about?" demanded Harper. "You said it was nothing, but you were weird about it last night and I want to know why. What did you do, Stu? What did you do? Is this like last time? You get into a fight with some poor sod then go too far and hurt them?"

"That was one fight, and it was twenty years ago. Good god, woman, don't you even trust me?"

"I love you, and yes, I trust you, but I know you and I know you have a temper."

"Look at me! I'm a pot-bellied old man wearing a Motorhead T-shirt and need to see a doctor every month if I'm lucky. I'm not about to get into a fight with a lump like Dexter."

"What about Carter? You never liked him, and you hate the others too."

"I don't hate them. I just wish they'd play better music."

"You enjoy a bit of folk." Harper stepped forward, her demeanour calm, and smiled at Stu as she asked, "Did you hurt them, love? It's okay, you can tell me."

Stu's fingers flexed, and his head ducked down until his chin almost rested on his chest, then he raised his head, a fierce look in his eyes, and stammered, "I... It's not what you think. Dexter and the band had a..." Stu paused, clearly undecided what to say.

"Yes? Go on, love, you can tell me."

"It was just a... No, I can't." Stu shook his head, then turned and hurried off, leaving Harper alone in the woods. She watched him leave, then shouted out, "You come back here this instant. Stu, I mean it!"

Stu stopped, then spun, and with a huff, and his shoulders rounded, he shuffled back like a sulky teen being told yet again to pick up his socks and use the laundry basket.

"That's better," said Harper, not unkindly as she held out her hands for Stu.

I felt very voyeuristic spying on such private moments, but if Stu was going to admit to murder, then I had little choice but to watch and listen. Anxious sat by my side, head cocked, as keen as me to uncover the truth that seemed like it might be forthcoming.

"Sorry to storm off in a huff, but you should have more faith in me."

"Stu, I do, and I love you no matter what. You know that. Gosh, we had some wild times, didn't we?" chortled Harper.

"We sure did. We were a right pair of tearaways," agreed Stu with a grin.

"So, what happened with those men? What did you do?"

"I'm not discussing it any further. I don't want you to get into trouble, and I don't want to be in trouble either. I want no more mention of us arguing, or the issues I had with Carter last year. It's done, and they're gone, so you have to trust me on this, okay? If I say it's over and I am not to blame, then you have to believe me. Understand, I am not to blame."

They studied each other for so long I felt like I was watching a movie still, then Harper nodded, and whispered, "Okay, Stu," before she leaned forward and pecked him on the cheek.

Hand in hand, they walked back towards the pub, thankfully not in my direction.

"Blimey, Anxious. What do you make of that?"

My faithful companion cocked his head to the other side, wagged his tail, and focused on my pocket.

Frowning, I fished around and found a rather fluff-covered dog biscuit. Laughing, I handed it over; he deserved it for being so good.

So, not only had Stu argued, possibly worse, with Dexter, but with the members of Freaky Fiddlers too. He hadn't admitted outright to killing the men, but he'd certainly come close. Was this enough to inform the police? Not really, as there was clearly no evidence and he hadn't been anywhere near the jars that evening, but as Ronnie had said, anyone could have tampered with them earlier in the day. Was this an ageing rocker out for revenge?

I needed some distance from this, and I needed to spend time with those I loved. Stu's involvement was something to consider, but without a real admission of guilt all I had was suspicions and an overheard conversation.

As I made my way back to the pub, taking a different route so I was sure not to bump into Stu and Harper, I found that things were starting to come alive. Abe and Gav were outside the pub talking with Ronnie, Meat was picking up litter where the stalls had been, Pat and the other two stallholders were dismantling the gazebos they'd left up last night, and the door was open to my campervan. Min was sitting in one of the chairs, a cup of coffee in her hands as she watched the goings-on.

I bypassed everyone, taking a wide berth to the camper, as I wasn't in the mood for talking without a proper coffee.

"Morning," sighed Min, smiling weakly as I returned. "And good morning to you, Anxious." She laughed as he launched into her lap and began licking. "Mind the coffee!" she giggled, then he jumped down, morning greeting accomplished.

"Morning," I said. "How come you look beautiful, and I look like a scarecrow in the morning?"

"Thank you for the compliment, but I don't feel beautiful. Especially after three hours of sleep. Is that right?"

"About that, yes. Two more than I managed. I had to sleep outside as you lot were snoring."

"That wasn't me!" Min winked, and smiled, then stood and asked, "Coffee?"

"Yes please. I had one with a detective earlier, but it wasn't great."

"Was she pretty?"

"Not as pretty as you. It was that O'Connell woman. Dolores."

"So definitely pretty. You know you could have your pick of women, right? You're handsome, have a fit body, lovely eyes, incredible tan, and more women appreciate the rugged look now so your long hair and beard are a real turn on."

"Really?" I asked, not sure if she was joking or not.

Min handed me my coffee after she turned off the gas on the stove, then frowned at me. "You never have got it, have you? You genuinely don't know?"

"Know what?"

"That you're a good-looking man and any woman would be lucky to have you."

"Don't make fun of me."

"Max, I'm not. I have told you before, but you always brushed it off. You're funny, smart, kind, and handsome. Most guys let themselves go, but if you get even a few pounds overweight you deal with it. By the time most men are your age, they're starting to sag."

"I'm only thirty-three!"

"Exactly. But you're like your dad, although don't let him know I said so. He's in his fifties and keeps himself in shape. He isn't overweight, and he's fit. You'll be the same."

"Then I thank you for the compliment. And I'll be sure to pass that on to Dad."

"Don't you dare," hissed Min with a killer glare and a jab of the finger for luck.

"Just messing," I laughed, sinking into the chair. "So, you think I'm handsome?" I asked smugly.

"Very. But that doesn't mean you aren't annoying."

I winked, then sipped my coffee gratefully. Nothing tastes better than your own coffee, especially when drunk in such good company. After chatting quietly about this and that for a while, I explained to Min about my early morning conversations and what I'd overheard by the river. She was instantly animated, and glanced around nervously in case Stu and Harper suddenly appeared, but they were outside their large motorhome and having a morning cuppa like us.

I was slightly jealous of the built-in retractable canopy they had. The colourful stripes added real cheer to the otherwise drab, beige vehicle, and was perfect on hot days for the shade it offered. Maybe I could get one added? But that would ruin the look of the VW and I had the sun shelter anyway.

"I would have never marked them as such hellraisers. You're sure the detective was talking about them?"

"Absolutely. And it's true about Ronnie and his buddies. They aren't so tough after all. What should I do about what I heard Stu say?"

"Nothing. Stay out of it. This is worse than the other times. Everyone might be in real danger here."

"I know, and that's why you should leave. Have breakfast then go home. You were going today anyway, so head off early and then I'll know you're safe."

"That's very sweet, but I'm staying. How will I know you're safe if I leave?"

"Because I'm invincible?" I asked.

"Seriously, Max, I'll hang around. We had such a lovely time yesterday until it went wrong, but now we need to find out who did this. People are scared."

"They should be. And so should you."

"And you."

"Trust me, I am. Min, I'd love you to stay, but you really should leave."

"No, not this time. Last week I was left out of it when you confronted the killer, but this time I'm going to be there. I want to be."

"Got the bug, eh? Max and Min the poisoned pickle police."

"Don't make fun of me!"

"Hey, I wasn't. I was just trying to lighten the mood. I'd love you to stay, but we need to be very careful, and we will have to speak to plenty of people to figure this out. Let's start with the stallholders."

"What were their names again? I remember the woman was Pat, but can't recall the others."

"Neither can I," I admitted. "They kept so quiet yesterday and weren't very memorable, but we should have remembered."

"There were too many others as well. All new faces, and I was more focused on the table full of dodgy looking men who turned out to be upstanding local business owners."

"What's all that racket out there?" crowed Mum from inside Vee, then proceeded to bang about like a rhino in a tiny camper, cursing under her breath and berating Dad for still being in bed.

"We're just chatting," I called, smiling at Min. I cringed as something cracked, and hoped she wasn't ruining over fifty years of van history in a single morning. Since when had I grown so attached to Vee? I think it must have been love at first sight!

"Then whisper. I didn't get a wink of sleep thanks to this tiny bed, and your father was snoring like an angry walrus."

"I was not. And how do you know what an angry walrus sounds like?" grumbled Dad.

"Because I live with one. Stop moving, you made me smudge my make-up."

"I am nowhere near you, and why do you have to do that now?"

"Because I really need to have a pee, and I am not going to be seen before I have done my face."

It went on like that until Mum was finally presentable enough to be out in public. She'd always been the same, and wouldn't emerge from the bedroom in the morning until she was fully ready for the day, even though it was just me and Dad in the house and he saw her before make-up was applied.

"Wow, you look amazing," gushed Min as Mum stepped down from Vee, resplendent in her red high heels, white dress with multi-coloured polka dots, her red hair held back by a white and black bandana and her make-up perfect. Even her lips matched her shoes.

"Thank you, my dear. At least someone knows how to appreciate the effort I put in."

"Hey, I do," I protested.

"Me too," called Dad as he staggered out, pulling on his white T-shirt then hitching up his jeans and fastening the buttons of his Levi's 501s.

Mum tsked, then hurried to the pub and spoke rapidly to Ronnie before rushing inside.

"I love that woman," said Dad, shaking his head. "But I gotta go too." He chased after Mum, waddling like a duck.

"Let's go and talk to Pat and the others," suggested Min.

"Okay, if you're sure?"

"Yes, I am." Min stood with her arms folded across her chest. I knew better than to argue. I used to argue. I always lost.

Anxious pined at his bowl, so I sorted him out some breakfast then left him to eat while we wandered over to Pat and the two men.

"Hi. We thought we'd come and see how you're doing. And sorry, but I don't think we got your names," I said to the two men sipping drinks now the gazebos were folded down.

"I'm Jake, this is Tim."

"Hi," said Tim.

"Hi. So, how are you holding up? Pat, are you okay?" I asked as she joined us.

"I am so not okay. I didn't sleep a wink, and those detectives were so rude."

"Pat, they were just doing their job," said Jake with a roll of his eyes.

"I saw that."

"You were meant to. You gave everyone a hard time when they were just asking questions to try to discover who killed two men."

"And they insinuated it was my pickled onions that were to blame, meaning me."

"It was your onions. And they didn't accuse you, they asked you questions just like they asked us. We got more grief than you. A sweet old lady, or two guys in their forties. Who do you think they suspected the most?" asked Jake.

"Less of the old," warned Pat. "Sixties is the new fifties, I'll have you know."

"But they said you were in the clear?" asked Min.

"They said we were free to go, yes? Why, you don't think they should have?" asked Tim, stepping forward in a very confrontational manner.

I was about to intervene, when Min put a hand to my arm then spun on Tim, took a step towards him and snapped, "With an attitude like that, then I'm not so sure. Who the hell do you think you are, trying to intimidate me? We all saw how you just acted. You better back off right now."

Tim went beetroot and shuffled backwards, getting angry looks from both Pat and Jake.

"That was not cool, mate," hissed Jake. "What's your problem? She was just asking you a question."

"I'm done with answering any more questions. I am out of here and good riddance to the lot of you. I'm going home. I should have gone last night, but I was too shaken up and had one too many beers."

"We all did, and were very upset. But yes, time to go."

"Agreed," said Pat.

"Are you allowed?" I asked. "Don't the police want you to stay around? I thought you lived miles away?"

"What? No, we live in the village. It's not far at all," said Pat, confused.

"Oh, sorry, I could have sworn someone said that you travelled around selling pickles and that you lived in your vans like I do. Like Stu and Harper."

"Well, we don't. Not all the time, anyway. I travel sometimes in the warm weather, but I do have a proper home," said Pat, seemingly affronted by the very idea she lived in her van permanently.

"We're the same. We live locally but sometimes use the camper to stay at festivals. It makes it easier. We were selling the pies and pasties and the pickles and onions and a few other things. We make good money, but we have to cook it all so go home to bake then travel for a few days to festivals."

"Oh, right. Well, it was nice meeting you all," I said cheerily, not really meaning it as I didn't get a good vibe from any of them.

With a few halfhearted pleasantries from them, Min and I left and returned to the campervan where Anxious was sitting watching his bowl with utter focus, hoping that for the first time ever it would submit to his command and refill.

"Keep on trying, buddy. It'll happen one day."

He glanced around quickly then his attention shot back to his bowl just in case he missed it happen.

"I don't trust any of them," said Min, slumping into a chair.

"I'm not so sure. I didn't like them, but I don't think they did it."

"But why? They were Pat's onions, and the other two weren't too friendly and kept very quiet all through what happened yesterday."

"Because they were freaked out. I'm not saying I'm right, just that they seem too close to this so I would rule them out because it would be very obvious. Their stock was confiscated, everything will be tested, and you can bet the police will have them in for more questioning. But let's see what the day brings. Maybe we'll change our minds."

"I agree. Now, are you going to make me breakfast, or do I have to starve? And what's for dinner? We need to have a real sumptuous feast to celebrate being alive."

"That sounds like a wonderful idea. Especially if you're staying for dinner?"

"I am staying until this is finished," said Min, actually stomping her foot to prove how determined she was.

"In that case, it will be lovely to have you here for another day."

We set about making breakfast, working together in that familiar way, our worries forgotten, if just for a while.

Chapter 11

Mum and Dad returned holding hands and laughing and joking with each other as they spoke quietly. They often shared little jokes and were always rather handsy with each other. I'd always find them whispering like kids and Dad guffawing at their private jokes like they were newlyweds, not seasoned veterans of the ups and downs of marriage.

"They're so sweet," said Min with a wistful sigh as we watched them approach.

"They've been together so long, but still love each other so much."

"Max, do you think that we could ever... No, sorry, forget it."

"Hey, it's alright. I get it. And yes, I do think we will."

"A year at least, remember? I want at least a year to rediscover myself and learn what it's like to be Min, not Max and Min. To do what I want, go where I want, not answer to anyone. To make sure you're really who you seem to be now, not an impostor."

"And I told you already, we have all the time in the world. There's no pressure, and I'm not pushing for anything, but you have to admit, for a woman trying to distance herself from her ex, you sure do spend a lot of time with me. One day, Min. You lasted one day then came with my folks to check out what I was up to."

"That was only because I didn't think it was real. I couldn't picture you out here in your campervan, so had to come see for myself. Make it real, if you get what I mean." Min smiled, bashful at my teasing.

"Again, I get it. I'm happy to have you here whenever you want, and so is Anxious."

Anxious barked his agreement.

"What's for breakfast, Son? I'm famished." Dad studied the prep area, nodding in satisfaction as he spied the makings of an epic fry-up.

"You need to watch your weight," warned Mum. "I don't want you getting a fat belly. There's nothing worse than a chubby rocker with a tucked-in white T-shirt."

Dad patted his perfectly flat stomach and said, "No fear of that. We've got dancing tonight, remember? So I can eat all I want today and burn it off later."

"We can't leave today!" declared Mum, aghast.

"Why not?"

"Because of these two." Mum pointed at me and Min like she could have been talking about anyone.

"What about them?" asked Dad, eyes switching between sausages and Mum.

"Yes, what about us?" I asked.

"They need looking after. Max here keeps getting involved in all these murders, but this time we're here to look after him. Silly boy." Mum wagged a finger at me.

Dad shook his head and shrugged, as if saying, what could you do?

"I don't need you to look out for me. I'm a capable man who just so happens to have helped figure out why people have been getting killed. I do fine on my own, thank you very much."

"Yes, until you don't. Then it will be his fault." Mum glared at Dad, daring him to disagree.

"You daft spotty lump," grumbled Dad. "He's a grown-up with his own life. He doesn't want us hanging around all the time. Leave him be. And there's no room in the campervan. You hated it in there. Your make-up area is bigger than Max's home."

With hands firmly planted on her hips, Mum locked her eyes on Dad until he wilted like a flower in a heatwave. He grumbled something incoherent, then suddenly found Anxious in need of a head rub so bent to hide his concern.

"Did you just call me a daft spotty lump?" asked Mum, voice light and sweet.

Everyone took a step away, even Anxious, leaving Dad stroking air. "No. You must have misheard," he mumbled.

"Good, because if you want to go dancing, you better not have said what I know for a fact you said."

"But if you know he said it, why are you saying he better not have?" I asked, winking at Min.

"Just make me my breakfast," ordered Mum, then disappeared into Vee and began clattering about. "How do you live like this?" she shouted out. "There's no surfaces. I need surfaces. And I can't even twirl to check my dress is hanging right."

"Your dress is fine," shouted Dad, almost bursting my eardrum.

"Where do you put your clothes?"

"I use the little cupboards. And it means I stay organised. At least I was until you messed up my systems."

Mum popped her head out of the open door and asked, "What was that?"

"Nothing, just saying that it will be good to have a tidy up after you've gone."

"Coward," laughed Dad.

The banter continued while Min and I made breakfast, Anxious by our side. Once everything was plated, we settled out in the morning sun and enjoyed a hearty fry-up to start the day. It soaked up the booze from the night before, and everyone visibly relaxed as we ate. A slice of normality when the world whirled around us in all its madness.

"That was awesome," sighed Dad as he put down his knife and fork and patted his stomach.

"I warned that you'd get fat," said Mum, poking Dad's tummy.

"That'll go down in a few hours." Dad leaned back and closed his eyes, laced his fingers behind his head and said, "Ah, this is the life. You got it made here, Son. So, what's the plan for today?"

"I'm not sure. Hang around here, go for a wander to stretch our legs, check on things at the pub."

"Solve a murder," added Min with a sly giggle.

"Yes, maybe," I admitted. "We should talk to the other band members and sound them out. See what they have to say about Stu."

"What's this about Stu?" asked Mum.

Checking we weren't being overheard, I filled them in on the morning's encounters, then finished my breakfast while they mulled it over.

"He didn't do it," declared Mum, her word final.

"You don't know that," said Dad. "He seems shifty to me, and if he used to be into all sorts and has a violent side, then maybe he did do it. Revenge."

"No, he isn't the type. And, Max, you said yourself that he didn't admit to it. He just said he didn't want to discuss it with Harper any longer. That's not proof."

"I know, but it's worth bearing in mind, and it wouldn't hurt to ask the other band members if they saw or heard anything."

"There won't be any suspects left soon, though, will there?" asked Dad. "Ronnie's cronies have left, the stallholders are packed up and will be leaving, so who does that leave that you can even talk to?"

"Just everyone who lives in the pub and the band members. Oh, and Barry, that sneak. I didn't get the chance to find out why he's being paid to follow me."

"I totally forgot about that!" said Min. "Who would do that? And why?"

"I have no idea. But I'm going to find out today."

"So if the suspects are leaving, how will you figure this out?" asked Dad, clearly genuinely interested. "And what about everyone who left before the poisoning? There were quite a few at the lock-in and hundreds of people before that. Could be anyone."

"That's a good question. But there's nothing stopping us leaving the pub and going to check things out in the village. In fact, how about it? We could all go and have a wander around Boar."

"See, I told you it was the name of a pig!" gloated Mum as she poked Dad's belly again. "That's why we got lost. You said it was Donkey."

"It's still an animal," said Dad, frowning.

"You got lost because you were looking for a place called Donkey?" I asked, trying not to laugh. "Since when are villages called Donkey?"

"Since when are they called Boar? What's that all about?"

"No idea? It's a Welsh thing. Most places start with Cwm, so maybe it means something else in Welsh."

"And don't forget that lots of towns and villages have two names. The Welsh one and the English one that's just a rough translation," said Min. "It's very confusing."

"And all the signs are in Welsh and English. How are you supposed to know where you're going?"

"Read a map? Listen to the directions on your phone? Follow the signs?" I offered, unable to keep it in any longer and laughing.

"Yeah, well, we got here, didn't we?" said Dad.

"See what I have to deal with?" crowed Mum. "He's a lost cause."

"I'm not the one who sent us down to the coast when we were meant to be heading inland to the country," snapped Dad. "You sent us in utterly the wrong direction, then got angry when I pointed out you had the map upside down and we weren't even on the road you were following."

"Then how about I drive us into the village later and we can have a wander around, maybe even stop by the florists?" I suggested.

"That's very sweet of you, love, but we do need to get back. Yesterday didn't turn out quite as expected, and we had planned on going home last night."

"Except we didn't even arrive until the evening," huffed Dad.

"Hey, we had fun," said Mum. Everyone just gawped at her. "Until poor Carter got poisoned and died in front of us," she added. "But it has been lovely." Again, we just gawped. "Apart from the death thing. Shall we go?" she asked brightly, seemingly over her concerns.

"We need to clear everything away, do the dishes, and sort out the campervan first," I reminded her.

"Great! I can help."

Min and I exchanged a look, then Dad intervened and said, "Why don't we take Anxious for a walk and leave these two to it?" He nodded at me knowingly, and I mouthed a silent thanks as Anxious began his usual insane yipping and ran circles around them in anticipation.

"You know you aren't meant to use the W word in front of him," Mum scolded.

"I know. So now we have to do it."

With a quick change of shoes for Mum into something more appropriate, they headed off, leaving us to tidy things up and get some order in place.

"Donkey!" laughed Min once they were gone.

"It's amazing they ever get anywhere," I said. "You okay with us going into the village? I don't think it's very big, but it might be fun. We could do with a change of scene."

"Sure. I think that will do us the world of good. And are you alright about me staying on?"

"Absolutely. I'm concerned about anything happening, but as long as we're together I'm sure we'll be fine. I do need time to process everything though. My head was so foggy last night that nothing's really sunk in yet."

"Ah, you need to let the clues present themselves," said Min knowingly.

"Something like that," I admitted.

"Max, don't put too much pressure on yourself though."

"How'd you mean?" I asked as Min handed me a plate and I dried it then placed it straight into the clear plastic box reserved for crockery. It was a small thing, but the systems I was slowly putting in place made me happier than I'd expected.

"I mean, I know you feel like this is your calling now, travelling around and solving crimes, but you have to think of yourself too. There are detectives and any number of specialists working on this, so don't be too hard on yourself. Relax, enjoy life. I know it was awful and very concerning, but truthfully it isn't your problem or your job."

"Min, I do know all that. I appreciate you saying it, but actually I'm feeling very calm and content. I'm not putting myself under any pressure. I know it isn't my responsibility, I know I might not end up helping, but I want to try. I do think this is some kind of cosmic fate at work here. That my life has been given a new and important purpose, but I'm not kidding myself either. Some you win, some you lose. All a man can do is be true to his heart and strive for happiness for himself and those around him. That's enough, right?"

"Oh, Max!" Min dropped the washcloth into the blue bowl of soapy water and flung herself at me. Her body vibrated as I held on to her and I felt dampness on my chest, her five five versus my six one meaning I could rest my chin on her head.

"Hey, what's wrong?"

Min pulled back and looked up, eyes and cheeks damp. "Why did you have to go and be such an idiot when you're such a beautiful man deep down inside?"

"I wish I knew the answer to that one," I admitted. "I get obsessed, consumed by things, and it ruined everything. But I'm trying, Min, I truly am. I'm forcing myself to take a step back from things if I get too single-minded, and it's working. I'm sorry."

"I know you're trying your best, and it's so lovely to see. I just wish.... No, never mind. Sorry. Come on, let's finish the dishes then maybe I can get cleaned up too. Will Ronnie let us use the shower?"

"Yes, he said it's no problem. There's one upstairs, a guest bathroom for people if they stay over and for the campers to use. He said it's fine."

"Great, then let's get showered and go shopping."

"Together?" I asked, a wicked smile spreading.

"Shopping, yes. Showering, no." Min flicked the tea towel at my legs then handed it to me and we finished the dishes.

While Min went to get clean, I pottered about in the outdoor kitchen loading the boxes, sealing the lids, stacking everything, then wiping down the fold-out table I used for meal prep. I liked the little routines, the way I was slowly getting into a groove with everything, and cooking and eating outdoors was a real revelation. Sure, everything took longer and was a hassle at times, but it made it an event, and allowed me to remain part of the world. Outside, and just present. In winter, such a life would be very difficult, but in a strange way I was looking forward to the challenge.

My beautiful VW campervan was an utter nightmare inside. How had Mum managed to wreak such havoc in such a short space of time? It was rather concerning. Mum was definitely not cut out for tiny home living. I gathered up her discarded clothes, folded everything, put her belongings back into her make-up bag, collected the bottles of perfumes, sprays, and various other items I wasn't sure of as to purpose, then stacked everything neatly by the door before folding back the bed and sitting, just to gather myself.

What would the police be doing now? How would they be trying to solve this? Were the detectives sitting behind their desks going over the scant evidence, or would they be more hands-on? If they'd spoken to everyone but hadn't actually taken anyone in under suspicion, then what was there for them to do? Would they be back around to speak to people again? I suspected they would, and most likely they'd call on those who had left, but unless someone outright owned up, what did they have to go on?

And what about me? What were my thoughts? Jumbled, I had to admit. Stu was clearly suspicious, but beyond that I was at a loss. If it wasn't Pat, even though they were her onions, then maybe it was one of the other makers? I'd hardly spoken to them, and that would have to change. Maybe there was something going on between them all and this was a simple way to discredit her. But murder over onions and a few pies and chutneys? They took it seriously, that was evident, but stooping to murder to get rid of some healthy competition was pushing things a little too far.

No, there had to be something else. Another motive, but that didn't rule anyone out.

"Okay, first piece of business. Sort that damn Barry out once and for all."

Determined, I marched across the grass towards where Barry had been staying then stopped, searching the edge of the small field in case I'd got the location wrong. I knew I hadn't, and cursed under my breath as I accepted that once again this strange man had disappeared. "Where's he gone now?" I muttered.

"Hey, looking for the weird brown guy?" asked Abe, one of the Freaky Fiddlers.

"Yes, but it looks like he's left."

"He drove off a few minutes ago. You should have seen him. It's like the guy didn't understand how a tent worked. He just bundled it into his Volvo without taking the poles apart or rolling up the tent and scarpered. Bit suspicious, right?"

"He's a suspicious kind of guy. But never mind, he'll turn up again. Sorry about your friend Carter. It was a terrible thing."

Abe flicked limp, thinning hair over his shoulders and teased the split ends as his eyes lost focus. "He was a great fiddler, and a great pickled onion eater. I just can't understand why anyone would do such a thing. What's the point? And why be so cruel?"

"I wish I knew. Was he having any problems with anyone?"

"Nope. We got on just fine, and have been travelling together for years. We live in the van for months with each other as we tour the local circuits, hit the festivals, that kind of thing. It's a tough life at times, but we enjoy the music and the people, and little events like this are a way for us to unwind. Takes the stress off, and lets us have fun rather than worrying about money."

"You don't get paid?"

"For gigs like this? Nah, it's just as a favour to Ronnie."

"Why do him a favour? Surely you need to earn money?"

"Ronnie was an old friend of Carter's. He knew him from back in the day, apparently. He was a little older than me, but younger than Ronnie, but knew him for a while before he upped sticks and moved here. We all like Ronnie. He's a good guy and fun."

"But Carter didn't have any issues with him or anyone else?" I asked again.

"Us three guys got on each other's nerves, sure. Being cooped-up in a van means that's inevitable, but we were real close and like brothers. Now it's just me and Gav, I'm not sure what we'll do. It won't be the same without Carter."

"I'm so sorry."

"Gav's talking about going back to South America. That would suck."

"South America?"

"Yeah, he's into the whole tribal thing, right? Spent a year out there with the indigenous people. Living like them, running around in a loincloth. He's fanatical about rainforests and environmental issues, which is why we're always skint," laughed Abe. "But listen to me rambling. I need to get a few things sorted, and I need to go and see his folks. The police will have told them, but it's best they get the full picture from me. I've been putting it off, but it's time to get back to the village and speak to them. We'll go home after lunch."

"Good luck. That's a difficult visit to make."

"It sure is. Nice meeting you properly, Max, and I hear you're quite the amateur sleuth?"

"I try my best."

"Then please figure this out. To be quite frank, it's got me really spooked. What if I'm next? What if we all are?"

"I hope you're wrong. Abe, how come you haven't gone home if you live locally?"

"We were hoping this would all get sorted, you know? We've hung around to see if we can help out, but I'm at a total loss. And we both wanted to keep our families out of this. Make sure they're safe. Mostly, we just don't know what to do. We like Ronnie, so figured we should stay."

Abe returned to the large, battered old motorhome and shut the door.

Annoyed Barry had vanished, I wandered back to Vee and found Min getting changed, so went to freshen up and hopefully have a pleasant day with my family.

Chapter 12

With Min and Anxious beside me, and Mum and Dad in the back, I drove along typical winding Welsh lanes, constantly on the lookout for unexpected temporary traffic lights and cones narrowing the road for no obvious reason. It seemed to be a particularly Welsh thing, this obsession with roadworks congestion but no actual roadworks.

After navigating a few hairy climbs and claustrophobic dashes along lanes only just wide enough to squeeze through, fighting down rising panic about having to reverse as I still hadn't had much practice in the van, we emerged onto a wider road and followed the signs for Boar, spelt the same in both Welsh and English.

"See, that isn't too difficult to follow, Dad," I called over my shoulder, catching him scowling in the rearview mirror.

"Your Mum sent us the wrong way," he said, shaking his head at being reminded.

"Not to worry, we're here now," I said brightly. "Look over there! They've got a bowling green right in the heart of the village. How cool is that?"

"I do love a game of bowls," said Dad, cheering up.

"Me too," I admitted. Min turned, eyes rolling. "What?"

"I have never in my life heard you mention bowls, or show any interest in the game whatsoever. And it's for old people, isn't it?"

"Don't be so prejudist," shouted Dad.

"Yeah, that's not cool, Min," I tutted.

"But it's true."

"I'll have you know that it's a recognised sport, and all the best players are in their thirties," huffed Dad.

"Then I'd love to see you guys have a game," said Min.

"Um, I haven't played for years," I admitted. "I might be a bit rusty."

"Me too," hollered Dad.

"No need to shout. You aren't in a different vehicle," I said.

"What was that?"

With a roll of my eyes, and Min stifling a giggle, I pulled up at the curb where there were a few spaces and turned off the engine.

We spent a few minutes reading a faded tourist information sign, coming to the conclusion that Boar was not a roaring metropolis, but a very small, ancient village with little more than a pretty high street, several side streets, a bowling green, a post office, a pub, and nothing much else. What made it special was that the population had remained a constant 1107 when they counted on a particular day in June for the last 49 years. There would be a big jubilee to celebrate the fiftieth anniversary, and it attracted a great deal of tourists because of it.

"How is that even a thing?" asked Min.

"When do they check?" asked Dad. "Bit weird, isn't it?"

"They check in June, in a few days. So not long from now," I said, squinting to read the tiny print, obviously in both Welsh and English. "It says lots of tourists come to celebrate and people visit at all times of the year because Boar is said to have special properties. Lots of groups interested in the supernatural and that kind of thing."

"Hippies and new age nonsense believers, you mean?" said Mum.

"That's very judgemental, and what's wrong with being a hippy?" I asked.

"Nothing, as long as you don't go out wearing your Crocs." Mum blanched, and unable to stop herself, her eyes lowered as she reluctantly checked what I was wearing. She sighed with relief as she found I was in trainers, not Crocs.

"These do, will they?" I chuckled.

"At least I don't have to pretend I don't know you. Come on, let's go and have a wander around. Maybe get a coffee."

The high street was a pleasant collection of antique shops, cafes, old-fashioned ironmongers, and tiny places that were locked up and by appointment only. Plus, of course, a Reiki healing place, three nail salons, two hairdressers, and a bookstore.

After an hour, we'd completed the tour and Mum had bought a wooden keyring with *50 years of 1107* burned into it, a commemorative plate of the small church with 1107 highlighted in gold around the edge, a wooden spoon from the antiques shop, and several packs of cards, again with the magic number emblazoned on them.

"What do you want that tat for?" complained Dad.

"It's not tat. It's cool stuff. There's something special about this place. There has to be. How can they possibly have the same number of people for so long?"

"Maybe nobody died and nobody was born," said Dad with a shrug.

"Don't be daft, you pilchard," scoffed Mum.

"I am not a pilchard."

"You are. Look, there's a lady pushing a pram, there's two old people who might croak it at any moment, and there's another baby over there with his dad. Pilchard."

"It's just lucky then," said Dad, sulking at being called a pilchard as usually that was what he called other people. Suddenly, he turned, and grinned at Mum. "Ha, in your face! The number's wrong anyway, isn't it? Two people died last night, and that's proof it's just hogwash."

"Maybe it will change before they count again," mumbled Mum, snorting her contempt for being put in her place.

"Let's go around to the bowling green. There's a cafe beside the clubhouse, so we can sit and watch then maybe have a game after," I suggested.

"Good idea," said Dad, brightening.

We settled ourselves at a large table outside a quaint cafe. Clematis climbed the walls, an abundance of purple flowers spilling over the arbour, and pelargoniums lifted their scarlet faces to the intense sun. The sky was so raw and blue it seemed like a painting. Dad insisted on buying the drinks so we just sat there, content to watch the men playing bowls, grateful for the dappled shade.

The grass on bowling greens was always so short I never knew how they managed it, assuming it must be maintained with a special mower, and how on earth did they keep it so flat and stop moles ruining it? One of these days I might ask, but decided some things truly were best left as a mystery.

Dad returned with the drinks and set a tray down, but Mum scowled at him.

"What was that for?" he asked.

"You did it again, didn't you?"

"Don't know what you're talking about," he said, eyes focused on the bowling green.

"Oh yes you do. You insisted on waiting and bringing the drinks out yourself, even though they offered to serve them when they were ready."

"I don't like to be kept waiting and not know when I'll have my drink."

"But you had to wait inside," said Mum, exasperated as always by Dad's quirks.

"That's different. I can watch them make the coffees, but if I'm out here, how will I ever know? And besides, they're busy, so I was a help."

"They are not busy. There's only us out here."

"Everyone else is inside," said Dad, snatching a quick glance through the window then looking away hurriedly.

"On a day like this? You silly man."

Mum smiled at Dad and shook her head. He grinned back and they both laughed.

I squeezed Min's hand, trying to tell her that one day we'd be like them. She put pressure on my arm and smiled; she got it.

After our coffee, and with the old fellas having finished their game, I wandered over to the clubhouse with Dad and we asked if the bowls were for hire. They were, and at a very reasonable price, so we booked an hour and called for the ladies and Anxious to join us. He wasn't too happy about not being allowed on the perfect green, but dogs and grass mowed to perfection twice a day did not mix.

Dad rolled out the jack and went first, his shot way too heavy-handed, and his bowl ended up in the ditch surrounding the green.

"Rubbish," I scoffed, then preceded to make a shot so slow that it only got halfway to the jack. After a few more goes, we warmed up and soon the competition was really on. With words of "advice" from Mum, and "encouragement" like, "That was lame," or "You missed it," from Min, we nevertheless had a fun time and got closer each round to not making a fool of ourselves.

"My turn now," said Mum, rolling up imaginary sleeves, adjusting her bandana, and hefting a bowl.

"But you've never played, love," protested Dad. "I don't want you to look silly. And, er, it's usually men who play." He turned to the men sitting outside, watching, all leaning forward as Mum and now Min each hefted a bowl and we showed them the basics.

"I know how to roll a ball, even if it is a funny shaped one."

"It's called a bowl," I explained.

"Oh, thank you, Sherlock, because without knowing that I'm sure I wouldn't have a clue what to do!" Mum snapped.

"Suit yourself."

Dad and I stepped back and left them to it, joining the regulars by the clubhouse as we believed we deserved the right.

"You fellas weren't too bad for amateurs," said an old guy with a flat cap, a bulbous nose, and a deep tan. His accent was so strong, the Welsh tang so melodic, that it took a while for the words to filter through and make sense.

"They did good," agreed a very similar-looking man, his accent even stronger.

"Thanks," beamed Dad. "And now the ladies want a go."

"Nothing wrong with the women playing," said flat cap.

"That's right, it's a modern world now," agreed his buddy.

"Of course," said Dad, "but my wife can't even throw a ball."

"This is different," said flat cap. "We've watched all sorts come and go over the years, and you'd be amazed how some people take to it even if they're no good at other sports."

"Plus, we get to ogle some nice bums for a change, instead of a load of grouchy men with their arses hanging out of their Marks and Spencer's chinos."

"True," agreed flat cap.

Mum must have heard, because she crouched low and gave her bum a right wiggle, much to the delighted gasps of the old guys and a groan from me and Dad, then she rolled the bowl in a perfect arc and it curled in then stopped with a barely audible thunk as it kissed the jack.

"She's a natural," said flat cap's buddy.

"Better than me," said flat cap.

Mum and Min high-fived, then Min took her turn and repeated the bottom jiggle. The old-timers spluttered, and I worried for their health as Min's jeans were very tight and she was always trim, then she let loose with her bowl and it curled around, following the same trajectory as Mum's, and gently tapped Mum's ball out of the way, taking her place.

"Hey," shouted Mum. "You can't do that!"

"That's how you play," shouted Dad.

Mum pouted, then took her turn and knocked Min out of the way, then Min just missed and Mum gloated by doing a little jig before the game continued.

Dad and I watched in silence, incredulous, until the game was over. It had been very close, but Mum just won, and the women hugged each other in fine spirits, then skipped back to Anxious waiting by the cafe.

"That's what we need around here," said flat cap. "Some new blood to ensure we get more babies and keep the numbers as they should be."

"I'm afraid we're just visiting," I said.

"Shame."

"So the winning steak of 1107 is finally broken, I assume? After the deaths yesterday. Did you hear?"

"Aye, we heard. Terrible business. But it isn't broken. In fact, it's looking just about perfect as long as there are no more nasty surprises."

"How'd you mean?"

"Well, that was two deaths, right, but there was a baby born a week ago, and there's a local due any day now. She's already a few days late, but I hear she'll have the little dear soon enough. We have until the deadline, and if all goes well our numbers will be perfect."

"So if she gives birth in time, the golden jubilee can go ahead?" I asked.

"Maybe, or maybe not. We'll still be one person too many. But there are plenty of oldies around here. Like us. As long as one of us drops dead, we'll be all set," he cackled.

"Sure, I guess. Good luck with it, I think. But why does it matter so much?" I asked.

"It brings in the tourists. It's a real attraction. People buy the local water, the local food, flowers, plants, anything that comes from the ground or just about any old nonsense really. They think our little village is blessed."

"It is," said the other man.

"True, it is. It was sad about those men, but as one flower fades so another blooms," said flat cap with a sagely nod.

"Yes, well, nice meeting you both. Thanks for letting us play. I'll bring the bowls back over," said Dad.

"Leave them there. We'll have another game later. Enjoy Boar."

"We will," I said, catching up with Dad who was already making his way to the cafe.

Mum and Min were sitting at the table, faces flushed, eyes dancing with excitement after their game. They were also so overflowing with smugness that they were in danger of drowning.

"Yes, you were both amazing," huffed Dad, then dropped into a chair.

"You played like you were naturals," I agreed, smiling at them both.

"Thank you," they chorused.

"You've never played before?" I asked Min.

"No, but I got the hang of it really fast. It's fun. I don't know why you two had such a problem hitting the little white ball thing."

"It's called a jack," grumbled Dad.

"Don't be sour," warned Mum. "We can't all be good at everything."

"Now you've ruined bowls for me," Dad moaned.

"But we found something out," I said. "The old guys said a baby was born and another is past due, so that will mean there is still one too many people in the village for the number."

"But someone might croak it," said Mum. "They better, or my souvenirs will have the wrong number on."

"You shouldn't have bought them until after the jubilee," scoffed Dad.

Mum shot him a warning glare and he sank into his chair. "I bet someone will die. It's a special place."

"That's what they said. So the good luck for the village might continue."

"I don't call two men being poisoned good luck," said Dad. "And tell that to the guy you're willing to die so you've got a load of tat with the right number on."

"No, but it's nice there are babies," soothed Mum, patting his leg so he'd stop sulking.

"S'pose."

"Let's go and get some flowers for Ronnie," said Min. "It might cheer him up."

"I was just thinking the same thing," I replied with a wink.

"Oh, yes, I am an utterly stupid woman," said Mum, scowling at us.

"What are you on about?" asked Dad.

"These pair want to go and snoop at the florists that Harry bloke owns. They think I'm too daft to realise."

"Maybe we have an ulterior motive," I admitted. "But we don't think you're dumb."

"Of course not," agreed Min. "But it would be nice for Ronnie. And the pub still stinks of vinegar. Shall we go?"

"We'll wait here. You two go," said Dad.

"But I want to go too," said Mum.

"They'll do better without us tagging along. Leave Max to do his thing, and Min to help him. If we all barge in, Harry won't say a thing. He wasn't the talkative type anyway."

"Maybe you're right," said Mum, clearly reluctant. "Off you kids go then. Don't be long, as we want to get home before dark and it's quite a drive. We'll have some lunch before we leave."

We agreed to be quick, so left Anxious with them and set off to the florists.

Chapter 13

"We forgot to do the shopping for tonight. I am not missing another one-pot meal. Yesterday was alright, but it wasn't what I had planned. Pub grub isn't really my thing."

"I thought you surpassed yourself. It was tasty."

"Hey, you cooked!"

"I know. And thank you for pretending to enjoy your steak. I know I overcooked it."

"No, it was, er, nice?" I ventured.

Min giggled, her hair bouncing as her body shook with happiness. I had to resist grabbing her hand and swinging her arm back and forth, but I managed it somehow.

"Let's go see the gangster florist, then we can pick up a few things. There are plenty of nice delis and butchers. What did you have in mind?"

"I'm not sure. Something special. A real treat after what we've been through. We need to seriously unwind, and so far it's been a whirlwind. We haven't had the chance to put our feet up at all."

"It's a deal. We should buy some nice bread as well if there's any of the good stuff left."

"And we need to have lunch. We'll make a simple pasta salad when we get back with boiled eggs and maybe some pesto. How does that sound?"

"Perfect. Add in a cheeky glass of wine and I'm all yours." Min reddened, then spluttered, "I mean, er, I'll be happy."

"It's okay, I get it, Min."

We greeted the people that we passed, both locals and tourists chatting excitedly about the magic of the place and its strange number of residents, then paused outside the florists where beautiful displays as well as flowers in tubs waited to be purchased. The smell was incredible, almost overpowering, but as I pushed open the door it was like nothing compared to the assault on the nostrils inside.

As we entered, a smartly dressed lady in a two-piece white suit was saying goodbye to Harry. He looked utterly incongruous with his shaved head, square jaw, old blue tattoos across his forearms, and that unmistakable hard man vibe, but his voice was light, tone friendly, and they clearly knew each other well.

"I'll see you again next week, Harry," said the woman, then smiled warmly at us as I held the door and she left.

When the bell chimed as it shut, Min asked, "How can anyone get away with wearing a white suit? I can't keep a T-shirt clean for five minutes."

"She has a real gift," said Harry, voice monotone, no emotion on his face now his customer had left.

"You don't mind us popping in to get some flowers for Ronnie, do you?" asked Min, staying upbeat.

"Of course not. That's a sweet idea. He'll be grateful."

"How have you been today?" I asked. "It was a weird night and very long with the police and teams there."

"I managed a few hours kip when I got home, but they put me through the wringer, same as they did for the others. They take one look at our past and assume the worst."

"But they didn't arrest anyone, did they?"

"Nah, just tried to get heavy and a bit intense. I handled it fine. I'm an old hand at dealing with the cops. It is what it is." Harry shrugged, saying it was no big deal for him, playing up the tough gangster card when he and I both knew none of them were quite as well-connected or mean as they made out.

"What's going on, Harry?" I asked, getting straight to the point. "Who would do this, and why?"

"Beats me. I'm just a florist."

"A florist with history. Could it be someone from Dexter's past that held a grudge?"

"Mate, those days are long gone. Most of those guys are either dead, in prison, or have new lives like us. And if they were out for us, it was very sloppy. Someone killed Carter on purpose, right?"

"It looks that way, but you never know. Maybe the onions got mixed up, or something else went wrong."

"Could be," he mused, rubbing his head as he frowned. "But it ain't likely. This was targeted. I think we all know that."

"Then what can you tell us about Dexter or Carter?"

"Look, you ain't the cops and I ain't here to answer all these questions. I've already been over everything with the detectives, and I'm not doing it again." Harry began sorting through flowers laid out on the work bench that divided the shop. He snipped off the ends of stalks expertly, the scissors incredibly sharp, then placed them in a vase of water one by one, eyeing them critically for balance of shape and colour.

"So, what would you suggest?" asked Min brightly.

"Suggest?"

"For Ronnie? What type of arrangement would he like? What will look best in the pub?"

"It won't matter about the pub, will it? He's shut down until they figure this thing out. Poor guy will be distraught. He'll be losing so much money. It better be sorted soon, though, what with the big celebration coming up."

"Oh, yes, we heard about that," said Min, whilst I remained silent as he clearly preferred talking to her than me. "It's rather strange, isn't it? Always the same number of people in the village?"

"Super weird," he grinned, laying down the scissors. "It started long before I arrived, but everyone around here thinks there's something to it. A bit of magic in the air, so to speak. It's awesome for business. I make a fortune. The tourists go nuts for anything grown here, and I sell a lot of live plants and make up these little bouquets with commemorative cards and they snap them up."

"So how come Ronnie doesn't hold the pickled onion festival around that time?" I wondered.

"That's because the producers, Pat and her cronies, do good business here in the village then. Ronnie tried to obtain permission to have something going on at the pub on the big day, but the local group of busybodies, those who organise the events, shut him down quick-smart. He was miffed, but what can you do? And anyway, it doesn't matter, because he makes a killing with drinks and food for a good few days before and after. It all works out."

"It is a very strange thing to happen," said Min. "But doesn't it make the place feel even more special?" she said brightly.

"Sure does! I love it here. Understand, I have found my home. I wouldn't do anything to mess that up. Look, guys, we might play up the gangster thing, but only because people like that edge, a bit of a story to tell, but honestly, we don't go around offing people with onions or any other way. Got it?"

"Sure, Harry, we get it," I said. "And thanks for being upfront with us. Now, let's sort out these flowers, shall we?"

It didn't take long for Harry to put something together, and we paid the extortionate amount for the flowers then left with him rubbing his hands together.

"I think we just got fleeced," I grumbled, my wallet feeling worryingly light even though I paid by card—that's how severe the damage to my bank balance was.

"I think you might be right. That will teach you to interrogate a suspect before you buy from them. You should have got the flowers then asked questions."

"True. And it's a lesson learned. Let's get what we need for dinner, then go and find Mum and Dad."

"Just don't pester the deli guy before we buy what we want," Min laughed, sniffing the flowers and sighing.

The deli was bustling, a true artisan shop that set my mouth to watering just looking through the window where various treats like quiche, pork pies, pasties, sausage rolls, cakes, and endless cheeses and meats were all displayed as a teaser for what promised to be gastronomic heaven inside.

"Hold yourself back or we'll be waddling around by this afternoon," warned Min, noting the look in my eyes. "I'm glad we didn't bring Anxious, or he'd be drooling worse than you."

"I'm not drooling," I protested, wiping my mouth and grinning. I let Min go through the door first, then followed on her heels, the smells divine.

We were served by two upbeat ladies more than keen to tell each customer how everything was made on the premises, that the meat was from the local butchers who only used the best of the best, and that people should be quick as by lunchtime they were usually almost sold out and they only stayed open until two.

Min and I took our time picking a few things, sampling much more, and emerged clutching nicely wrapped parcels placed carefully into a branded paper bag.

"Now I'm famished," groaned Min, clutching her bag tight.

"Me too. Let's get the meat and bread then go back to the pub. This will be a feast of a day." With my spirits lifted thanks to the promise of fine food and even finer company, Min and I stormed through the rest of the shopping, choosing some nice cuts for dinner and two fantastic looking loaves. One for lunch, the other for dinner or to keep for the next day if we suffered from bread overload.

Mum and Dad were itching to go, especially once we teased about the lunch we would have, so we hurried home—it still felt strange to call wherever I had pitched up my home!—and opened up Vee. I wanted to let the air flow as Anxious was still suffering from pickled onion fart syndrome and Mum and Dad were close to needing oxygen masks.

We piled out with relief, even Anxious desperate to get away from his own behind, and gasped as we sucked down the good air, not the utterly ruined forever stuff.

"Right, leave lunch to me," insisted Mum with that no-nonsense tone that made it clear there would be no arguments, and if there were she would win.

"Great, I'll go stretch my legs," said Dad with relief.

"You will do no such thing! I need you here to do my bidding."

Dad's shoulders sank as he mumbled about it not being fair, so Min and I beat a hasty retreat so Anxious could do what dogs needed to do way too often, then returned to the pub to check on Ronnie and hopefully cheer him up.

"Hey, Tanya, how are you doing today?" I asked as we breezed into the pub after ducking under the tape still stretched across the door. "I'm surprised Ronnie hasn't ripped the tape off by now."

"He wanted to, but I told him he shouldn't. At least not until later on. The police might come back, and the last thing we want is more trouble."

"True, but they've finished, haven't they?"

"I think so, but it was such a rush and so chaotic that I don't know what's going on." Tanya leaned her mop in the steel bucket and sighed as she tugged on her long ponytail and flexed her fingers to get some blood flowing. "Ugh, I'm shattered. This place was a right mess and the powder for checking for fingerprints gets everywhere. There are loads of weird smells, too, from the chemicals they used to test for anything nasty, and I've been at this for ages now."

"It's looking great though," said Min, checking out the shiny bar, the gleaming brass rails, the sparkling pumps, and the now spotless flagstone floor.

"Thanks. It was a lot of work. Can you still smell the vinegar?" Tanya retrieved a bottle of air freshener from the bar where she had a tub of cleaning supplies and spritzed the air then sniffed. "All I can smell is this stuff, but maybe it needs a few more squirts."

"No, that's enough," I spluttered, the haze of the spray making my face wet and my nose tickle. "The vinegar has gone, but any more of that stuff and it'll be even worse. We brought something better. Something to cheer Ronnie up." I nudged Min and she showed Tanya the flowers.

"Aw, that's so sweet. He'll like that. He's always enjoyed having flowers around the place. Bet Harry totally fleeced you, right?" Tanya winked, then chuckled.

"Utterly," I admitted. "I don't think he likes us."

"Don't take it personally. Harry doesn't particularly like anyone. Why he became a florist is beyond me, but you can't deny your passion, can you?"

"I guess not," I said, knowing just how hard that was. "When you get a calling, it's way too easy to let it consume you."

"He loves the flowers, the customers not so much. But I think he's happy in his grumpy world, and he's good at faking it for the locals. They love the fact he's a hard man selling flowers. All the women are after him."

"Really?" I asked, surprised.

"Yeah, it's that menacing vibe. They love it. A bit of rough."

"He's certainly got that going for him," I said, nonplussed. "So, where's Ronnie?"

"Not sure. Around somewhere. Probably feeling sorry for himself in the kitchen. The police really pulled a number on him. They took everything. Trying to sort it out with the insurance is going to be a real headache."

"I'm sure he'll figure it out. But yes, they had to take the food because of the body in the freezer."

"I'll go get him. You cool to wait here?" Tanya didn't wait for an answer, and strolled down the corridor to get Ronnie.

"Did they have to take everything from the freezer?" asked Min.

"I know it seems like they went overboard, but you can't store dead people with food. It's just not allowed. Ronnie knew that, but he took a risk and it didn't pay off. I'm not saying it would make a difference to the meat as it was frozen and Dexter wasn't touching any of it, but it's simply not what's allowed in kitchens. I'm guessing he'll have to go through all kinds of hoops to get inspected again, and that's without the headache of restocking the food. It's a massive waste of resources, but the police can't let him take any chances."

"I suppose it makes sense. So you didn't keep any corpses in the freezers where you worked?"

"No, just heads," I laughed.

"Silly." Min grinned, but when Ronnie appeared we turned serious. We were talking about his friend, after all.

"What brings you two back here? Not another shower, is it?" he asked, seeming distracted. Ronnie sniffed, then asked Tanya, "You been going overboard with the air freshener?"

"Maybe a little, but at least the vinegar smell has gone." She gathered her mop and bucket and took them away. I wondered if she would use the broom closet or if it was too strange to go in there knowing what had happened. But I supposed she'd got everything from there to clean up, and she didn't seem the squeamish type.

"We came to give you these," beamed Min, pulling the bunch of flowers from behind her back where she'd been hiding them.

"Oh, that's so kind. Thank you. They look lovely."

Min handed Ronnie the flowers and said, "You're welcome. We thought it might brighten the place up a little. Something to keep your spirits up. How are you and Meat doing? Is he okay? I haven't seen him today."

"He's okay. He's been sorting a few things out, tidying up, but mostly staying out of everyone's way. It's hit him hard this morning, the daft lump, but he ain't one to show his emotions. Like me, I guess." Ronnie shrugged, then sniffed the flowers. I noticed a tear form before he turned away to lay the flowers on the bar. "I'll put those in water in a mo. You had a nice morning?"

"Great!" said Min. "We went into Boar and had a wander around, bought some nice food, and got the flowers."

"And Harry fleeced you, right?" Ronnie laughed.

"Utterly," I said. "No mates' rates for us."

"Harry doesn't do mates' rates. He charges whatever he thinks he can get away with. So, what did you think of Boar? It's a lovely village, eh? Quiet, but smart, with plenty of good people."

"Everyone was very sweet. We even played bowls on the green."

"And showed off how great you were at it," I said.

"Some people are just naturals. I never could get the hang of it," said Ronnie.

"And you never told us about the strange claim to fame the village has," said Min.

"I didn't? You mean the weird number of residents thing?"

"Yes. It's very exciting, isn't it?"

"I wouldn't go that far. It's just a gimmick for the tourists."

"But what are the chances of there always being the same number of people living here? I mean, people must come and go all the time."

"Actually, no, they don't. It's odd, but I think there have only been a few in all the years I've lived here. This is a peculiar place. It's why everyone still talks about me and the guys so much. We kinda saved the day."

"How so?" I asked, intrigued.

"When I moved here, they were still a few people down on the right number for that year. But then the other guys followed on up, this was after me, Meat, and Dexter had already arrived. The other three made it the right number and that year we had a massive celebration as everyone had been so worried they'd lose the status as the village that time forgot."

"So you got here just in time?"

"Yeah. It was a freaky time. Some of the residents really get into it. They believe it's very important. So when me and the guys said we were staying, and the number was spot on for the year, all the people who loved the claim to fame were all over us. Sending us gifts, making food, all that kind of stuff. They wanted us to stay. Said we were their lucky charms. It's stuck, I guess."

"And what do you think about it?"

"What I think is they should have let me have the festival here on the day they celebrate in the village. But I get where they're coming from. I still do really well out of it, which is why I'm so gutted about this place. I don't know if I'll be allowed to open in time, and in the meantime I'm losing money hand over fist."

"They'll let you open soon enough, Ronnie," I said. "I'm sure they will. Once the dust settles in a day or two. Just give them time to get everything straight, and hopefully catch who did this, then you'll be open again."

"I hope so."

"Ronnie?" asked Min, her voice tentative.

"Yeah?"

"How come people don't leave the village? I mean, what about the younger generation? Surely they must head off to do their own thing? Go to college, move away, get married, raise families someplace else? It just doesn't sound right that the numbers could always remain the same."

"Your guess is as good as mine," Ronnie shrugged. "Sure, the kids move on, get jobs in towns and cities, but it just always evens out with babies being born, or a few newcomers like me and the guys. But this year might be the end of fifty years of history. We don't normally get murders upsetting the apple cart."

"No, I bet you don't," I said. "But there was a new birth, and apparently another on the way. That still means you're one person too many, but who knows what will happen?"

"I guess. But it's the least of my worries anyway."

"Enjoy the flowers, and try to stay positive," said Min, smiling at Ronnie who acted like half the man he'd been.

"I'll try. And thanks. They look and smell lovely."

We left Ronnie just standing in the middle of his pub. He seemed to have lost his spark. He was tied to his pub and without it he was adrift on a sea of despair.

Chapter 14

"Wow!" I whistled as we returned to the campervan.

"You really went all out," said Min. "But I don't think I could eat even a fraction of it."

"Whatever we don't eat, you can save for later or tomorrow," said Mum.

"What about us?" asked Dad. "Don't we get to take some home? I'll be starving later."

"You didn't buy it," hissed Mum, slapping him on the forearm with a wooden spoon.

"Ow!" Dad rubbed his arm happily and eyed the spread greedily.

"You can take whatever you want with you," I laughed. "Mum, you didn't need to go to so much trouble. You could have just put a few things out on plates or in bowls."

"You know I like to do things properly. I miss not having my hamper, but this will have to do."

"I don't even recognise half of this stuff."

Mum had spread out our picnic on a chequered blanket, with the various nibbles, cold cuts, cheeses, sun-dried tomatoes, and more in nice bowls, with plates and cutlery for everyone. There were folded napkins, drinks, and even a few wild flowers to really make it look like a banquet.

"Well done, love. You do lay on a lovely spread." Dad kissed her and she beamed, always happy to be praised for a job well done.

"Sit down then. Let's tuck in."

Everyone, including Anxious, took a seat, and before the rest of us got our lunch Mum whispered to the keen pooch who immediately sat up straighter, eyes locked on hers. She set a bowl before him and rammed it with a sample of everything.

"Not too much," she warned him, completely oblivious to the amount of food already offered. "We don't want you getting fat. But as a treat, as long as that's okay?" she asked me.

"It's fine. We've been watching what we eat, so a treat won't do any harm. Although, I'm not so sure I'll be able to say the same thing after all this."

"I'm going to totally pig out then starve myself later," said Dad, hand reaching out for a thick slice of beef.

And so it began.

An indeterminate time later, we all groaned, moaned, sighed, or lay on our backs. Mostly we tried a little of each, rotating through until we settled on being prone and groaning. It seemed to work the best!

Once we'd recovered enough, Min and I packed everything that was left away, splitting it between us and my parents, much to Dad's relief and Mum's annoyance, then we washed up while Mum and Dad sorted out their things then relaxed.

Soon enough, it was time for them to say goodbye.

"Don't let him get into any trouble," warned Mum.

"I won't," said Min with a smile.

"And be sure to call when you have news," Dad told me.

"Sure thing. Drive safely, and put the route into your phone so you don't get lost."

"Don't you worry about that, Son. I've got it all up here." Dad tapped his head and everyone groaned.

"And I've got it on Google Maps, so we'll be home in a few hours," said Mum, tutting.

After a kiss and a hug, we waved them off and returned to the camper.

"Wow, it's so quiet without them here," noted Min.

"It's always been like that. They're like a gang of unruly children, not two adults. But they have a real lust for life, and that's good."

"It is. And they're so cute together."

"The one thing I would never describe my parents as is cute. Mad. Loud. Loving even. But not cute."

"Help!" screamed someone from the far end of the field.

"Is that Harper?" gasped Min.

"Sounded like her. Come on!"

Anxious began to bark, clearly sure something was up, and tore around the campervan with us racing to catch up.

"Somebody help me, please!" wailed Harper as we caught sight of her tearing at her fine hair and waving her arms frantically.

"What's wrong?" I shouted as we closed in on her.

"In there. It's... It's just awful. We need to do something."

At that moment, the door to the Freaky Fiddlers beat-up motorhome slammed open and Gav gripped the doorway, sinking to his knees, covered in a sheen of sweat, bright red, and urging.

"What happened?" asked Min as we passed Harper and went to help Gav.

Anxious yipped from the bottom of the steps, as if there might be someone dangerous in the motorhome.

"I knocked but nobody answered, so I opened the door and Abe and Gav were on the floor covered in sick and bright red. I thought they were both dead. Is Abe dead? What's happening? Have they been poisoned?" she asked as she hurried over to us.

"I have no idea. Let's just help Gav," I said as I reached out to steady him as he began to topple forwards. His grip was locked on the door frame, knuckles white, but his face was like a ripe tomato fit to burst.

"Come on, Gav, let us help you to get out," I soothed, trying to prize his fingers loose gently.

Gav was gurgling and his eyes were unfocused, but he turned his head and grimaced, although I think he was trying to smile. He opened his mouth to speak but nothing but a garbled moan escaped, then he slumped forward, all strength gone, his fingers losing their grip as he fell into my arms.

I staggered back under the unexpected weight, but managed to get my hands under his armpits and dragged him back before Min and Harper helped me to lay him on his side. His face was getting even redder, which I didn't think possible, and a nasty liquid was oozing from his mouth, but his eyes were open, and he was breathing, so I figured that was a good thing.

"What should I do?" asked Min, eyes panicked, body tense as she bent but didn't touch Gav.

"Go and get Ronnie and call for an ambulance. Check everyone else is alright. Who else is still here?"

"Just Ronnie, Meat, Tanya, me, and Stu," said Harper. "Everyone else has left."

"Harper, I want you to go with Min and find them. Where's Stu?"

"I don't know. He went for a walk after lunch."

"And is Abe inside the motorhome?"

"Yes, but he looked worse than Gav."

"Right, then first let's get him out here, then you two go and round everyone up and make the call."

We rushed into the motorhome, but it was clear that Abe was in a much worse state and even as I breezed through the door he took his final breath then was still. He was half-buried under an avalanche of books that had been on a long shelf on the far wall now hanging off the brackets. I couldn't help noting the bright images and titles, all seemingly of South American locations, definite bias towards rainforests and animals. Abe had been right. Gav really was into the indigenous peoples of the region and the flora and fauna.

We did what we could, but nothing brought him back, and we couldn't spend too much time trying as Gav needed us and it was clear nothing was working.

Min and Harper dashed off, Min already phoning for an ambulance, as I tried to make Gav comfortable.

"Can you speak? How are you feeling?" I asked as his colour subsided and he stopped the disconcerting gargling.

"I... I'm not dead?" he wheezed, voice raspy and barely a whisper.

"No, mate, you aren't dead. I think you came close, but my guess is you're over the worst."

"I bloody hope so. I've... never... felt so ill in my life." He hurried the last few words, then coughed, it clearly being too much effort.

"Stay still and the ambulance will be here soon. But can you tell me what happened? Was there someone here?"

"No... nobody. Just me and Abe. Is he..."

"Yes, I'm afraid he's dead. He didn't make it."

"Poor guy. We both felt weird after lunch, and then..."

"It's okay, no need to say anything else. You're going to make it. Hang in there."

Ronnie, Meat, Tanya, Min, and Harper arrived looking stressed and fearful, especially Harper.

"I can't find Stu," she said. "I called, but there's no sign of him. What if he's dead?"

"Or he's the one that killed them," said Meat, glaring at her.

"Don't be ridiculous!"

"We all know he's got a temper, and has fallen out with a few around here, but that's going too far, Meat," warned Ronnie.

"I was just saying what you thought. He argued with Dexter, he fell out with Carter, and I bet the other two as well, and now they're dead."

"Gav isn't," I reminded him.

Aware of how serious his condition was, everyone crouched so we weren't looming over the poor guy like medics studying a corpse on a gurney, and Ronnie asked, "How you doin'?"

"I'm alive. Barely. I feel so ill. Like my insides want to pop out, and my heart is beating way too fast. I think I might have a heart attack."

"Just lay still and breathe deeply," said Ronnie calmly, casting a concerned glance my way.

"The ambulance is coming, and they'll sort you out, no fear," said Meat, placing a large hand over Gav's and squeezing.

"Thanks, Meat, you're the best." Gav's eyes closed slowly and we held our breath, fearing he was gone, but then they snapped open, he coughed, and shot upright. "Abe's dead? Tell me this is a dream?"

"He's gone, mate," said Ronnie kindly. "We got here too late. Rest easy. Help's coming."

And to be fair, help arrived sooner than any of us could have expected. An ambulance tore into the pub car park and two paramedics jumped out, hurried over with large packs, and as we explained what had happened one got to work on Gav while the other went to check on poor Abe, who was, as we already knew, dead.

The paramedics explained that they'd just finished another call a mere mile away and got notified about us so rushed right over. They immediately put Gav on a drip and asked him endless questions, but Gav was hardly coherent and found it difficult to speak so they gave him oxygen, something to slow his heart rate, and then a sedative. He sank back and looked peaceful as the paramedics took a moment to ask us for details.

None of us knew what had happened, just that they'd seemingly been poisoned like the others, so we went to check in the motorhome and found the remains of their lunch. Nothing special, just half-eaten cheese sandwiches with an empty pack of ham from a supermarket still on the table.

"At least there was no pickle," noted Meat.

"Not cool, mate," hissed Ronnie.

"It's true."

"Can everyone go outside, please?" asked the paramedic. "We don't want to contaminate the evidence. This is four poisonings now, three of which have been fatal, so nobody touch anything. If I were you, I'd ensure that whatever you eat is only something you know is safe."

Outside, we watched as Gav was taken away on a stretcher and then the ambulance drove off, leaving us alone with the body of Abe on the floor of the motorhome.

"What do we do now?" asked Min as we gathered outside where Gav had lain.

"Wait for the police to arrive, I assume," I said.

"This is gonna bloody ruin me," sighed Ronnie, tugging at his lip so hard I worried he'd rip it off.

"Ronnie, two guys just died," warned Meat.

"One guy died, the other will make it. Hopefully," I corrected. "Gav seemed to be recovering, so maybe he didn't eat as much of his lunch as Abe."

"This is getting beyond strange," noted Ronnie. "Why is everyone being killed at my pub? What's being used to do it? And how are they doing it? Who's the sneak?"

"Hey, don't look at us," I said. "We just had our own lunch, said goodbye to my folks, and this happened."

"And me and Ronnie were inside with Tanya. We were together and have been all day."

We turned to Harper, who was fidgeting with her hair and looked ready to bolt as her neck flushed and her eyes wandered.

"Well, I didn't do it!"

"No, but where's Stu?" growled Ronnie. "And how do we know it wasn't you?"

"Ronnie, mate, it's Harper and Stu," said Meat, trying to calm him. "We know them both, and they ain't no killers. They've been coming here for years. They're good people. The best. They're like us."

"If they're like us, then maybe they did it. Maybe they want to discredit me, or maybe Stu's temper finally got the better of him. He's trouble, that one."

"Ronnie, how could you say such a thing?" gasped Harper. "We're friends. We come every year, sometimes twice, and we always have a blast. You know us. We would never do anything to hurt your business or you. Stu has a temper, but he's past all that violence. You know that. You know us."

"Sorry. I'm losing the plot here."

"I'm going to take another look inside the motorhome," I said, nodding to Min. "Are you okay to wait here?"

"Yes, of course. But don't mess anything up."

"I won't touch a thing. And everyone remember to be careful. We need to watch what we eat, like the paramedics said."

Entering the motorhome again was beyond strange. Having to step over Abe felt wrong, almost blasphemous, and I hated making him suffer the indignity even if he was gone. The bright colours of the books strewn across his body and the floor seemed surreal, like nothing should be cheery, and the fallen shelf was screaming at me to be repaired, but I stayed my hand and left everything as it was.

In our haste to save Abe, I'd paid hardly any attention to the table, but now had the time to study it properly. It really was just two plates with ham and cheese sandwiches, confirmed by the fillings and loaf still out on the L-shaped counter of the surprisingly large kitchen area that divided the rest of the motorhome.

I noted two glasses on the floor, both knocked over as the men became ill, the shelf clearly having been grabbed to steady themselves. What had they drunk? Could it have been that? I checked the floor, but there was nothing else that could have killed Abe, so moved deeper into the motorhome, checking out a small living area with a built-in sofa and a large TV. Various mementos of festivals and places they'd played were on shelves, pictures of the band on the walls, with hats, scarves, and badges pinned up to make the place a little brighter and more personal.

I carefully moved to the other end of the vehicle again, saying a silent sorry for stepping over Abe, then past the kitchen and checked in the bathroom, although I wasn't sure why. Everything looked as it should. Cramped, cluttered, but organised in the best way they could considering three men often stayed here for days or weeks at a time. I couldn't even imagine what that would be like, and it was a credit to them that they hadn't killed each other long ago. There must have been plenty of arguments. Living on top of each other would undoubtedly be hard, but they had their music and had seemed happy with their way of life.

There were two tiny bedrooms, at least by the standards of regular homes, but for a motorhome I supposed they weren't too bad. One held a single bed, the other two singles with a tiny space between them. I decided to check the single room first. My guess was this was Gav's as it held more books on South American countries, way too much information about frogs, a lot of pictures of tribal members with red face-paint and fascinating jewellery, and even a number of rough wooden statues presumably from his travels.

Clothes were folded in neat piles, various instruments were lined-up against a tiny desk which held a compact tablet, and as far as I could tell all was as it should be.

Moving into the other room, I squeezed between the unmade beds, marvelling at how two grown men could function in such a small space. There wasn't much to see, as there was no room for anything, but instruments had been cleverly hung on walls, there were several shelves with music and fantasy books, and two laptops on a shelf cluttered with aftershave, deodorant, and random things like pens, CDs, flyers for festivals and events I presumed they were to appear at.

Nothing stood out anywhere, and nothing screamed foul play beyond two of them now being dead and the other presumably in intensive care. Apologising to Abe yet again for stepping over him, I hurried outside and closed the door, happy to breathe untainted air, now concerned I might have inhaled something deadly, but certain it was what they'd eaten or drunk.

Everyone was still milling about, unsure what to do, where to go, so I asked the obvious question, "Shouldn't we try to find Stu?"

Chapter 15

Anxious pawed at my legs, gentle but insistent, so I squatted and encouraged him to cuddle in close and have a nice ear scratch. He whined a little, clearly perturbed by events. Two of his favourite people in the world had come and gone, then there had been the chaos with Abe and Gav, and the poor guy must have been very confused.

"It's okay, there's nothing to worry about. I'm here, and so is Min."

Anxious turned to look for her and she smiled then bent, making a fuss of him.

He wagged, happy as always when we were together.

"Were you feeling sad?" Min asked.

Anxious' ears lowered and he whined again, clearly not feeling right at all.

"He didn't eat anything, did he?" I asked, suddenly very afraid. I didn't know what I'd do without him, and couldn't imagine a life without the little guy by my side.

"Don't worry, Max, he knew something wasn't right and wouldn't go near Gav. He sat outside the motorhome while you were in there."

"That's a relief. How are you doing?"

"Utterly freaked out," admitted Min. "What on earth is going on in this place? Now sandwiches are being poisoned?"

"Either that or their drinks. I guess everything will be tested and we'll find out at some point, but this is now becoming too dangerous. Why would anyone be doing this?"

"Because they want to put me out of business," lamented Ronnie as he loomed over us, Meat by his side.

"It's rather extreme, isn't it?" I asked.

"Dunno," shrugged Ronnie. "But it'll work. Nobody will want to come here with a killer on the loose."

"Then we need to find who's doing this. It isn't safe for anyone, and who knows what's planned next? Ronnie, has anything strange happened in the pub?"

"Like what? I can't even open to sell beer, and I've been turning people away. Word will get out and I'll be ruined. But no, there's nothing strange going on apart from blokes turning up dead and corpses in motorhomes. You need to be very cautious. No eating or drinking anything unless you know where it came from and haven't taken your eyes off it."

"Good advice," said Min. "We should go to the shops and eat something right there and then or at a restaurant."

"Unless the poisoner works at the restaurant," said Meat brightly.

"Mate, not helping," hissed Ronnie.

Meat shrugged. "Just sayin'."

Min and I stood, and I said, "Let's find Stu first. Anxious, where's Stu? Have you seen him?"

Anxious sat and wagged, understanding something was about to happen, but not knowing what.

"Of course, you don't know the name." I called to Harper and she came over. "Have you got something of Stu's? Let Anxious smell it and he might be able to track him down."

"Yes, great idea," she said, eyes darting every which way, clearly hoping he'd just turn up. "I'll go and get something."

A minute later she returned with a faded Metallica T-shirt. I took it then encouraged Anxious to take a good sniff of the whiffy shirt.

"Sorry, it was in the laundry basket so is quite ripe."

"All the better for Anxious to get a real scent. Anxious, go find," I said, my voice light and cheery. "There's a biscuit for you if you find him." I pulled one from my pocket and waved it in front of him. He didn't need telling twice.

Nose to the ground, Anxious zig-zagged back and forth, weaving his way over to Stu and Harper's campervan, then he shot off towards the trees by the river.

We followed, racing to keep up as the smart Terrier snorted up the scent of Stu and seemed to know exactly where he was going. Min and I were in the lead, followed by Tanya, with Ronnie, Meat, and Harper wheezing in the rear, clearly not used to the fast pace.

Slowing at a dense thicket of trees, Anxious took a moment to orient himself, then, nose to the grass, he darted forward and began to yap.

Everyone caught up at a rickety bridge crossing the river and paused to catch their breath.

"Well done, Anxious." I gave him a biscuit as he'd done so well. He took it off to one side to eat in peace, while the rest of us paused to inspect the bridge.

"Is it safe?" Min and Ronnie.

"Yeah, sure. I don't ever tell anyone about it because it's pretty old and there's not much on the other side, but it's sturdy enough."

"Then we need to go over. One at a time?" suggested Harper, flustered and looking rather waxy.

"I'll go first," said Ronnie, then strode over without pause. "See?" he beamed, once on the other side.

We took turns, with Anxious whizzing across the moment I stepped foot on the bridge, then we turned to face the dense undergrowth and veritable forest of coppiced trees left to grow wild over the decades.

"Do you own this?" I asked Ronnie.

"It came with the pub. There's a lot of land, actually, but most is left to do its own thing. Apparently, this used to be coppiced regularly back in the day to feed the fire in the pub, but it hasn't been cut for a very long time. Looks nice, eh?"

"A proper old woodland," I agreed. "Should we follow the path?"

Ronnie shrugged, but Anxious knew what he had to do and after snuffling in the leaves and twigs, he soon picked up the scent and trotted along the path.

We followed at a thankfully more sedate pace, nobody speaking, everyone fearing the worst. The path weaved between the trees, making it difficult to see far. Nettles and viscous, thorny brambles snagged on our clothes and stung our hands until Ronnie picked up a slender branch and cleared the way. He forged ahead like a wild man of the woods, grunting with each swing, and clearly happy to release some pent-up emotion on the unsuspecting flora.

Anxious began barking from up ahead so Ronnie thrashed at the brambles, his solid frame making short work of even the thickest trailing meanies, and we charged ahead as Anxious' call became more insistent.

We burst into a clearing, Harper gasping beside me, looking terrified of what we'd discover, then stopped short as we spied Stu sitting on a rotten fallen trunk, his head in his hands, unmoved despite my buddy pawing at his legs. Then his head lifted, sunlight catching his thinning hair and making it shine, and he reached down and ruffled Anxious' head, who sat, tail wagging happily, then licked Stu's knee.

Stu laughed weakly as Anxious barked happily then raced back over to me and sat, eyes glued on my pocket, willing the biscuits to burst free into his already open mouth.

"Well done! What a clever dog you are." I handed over three biscuits and he settled against a tree, dropped them, then held one between his paws and took his time nibbling his treats, his work here done.

While this was happening, Harper had reached Stu and sat beside him, so we hurried over, concern and confusion writ large on our faces.

"What happened?" Harper asked Stu as she took his hand gently and stroked the back of it with her other. "I was so worried. Terrible things have happened and I couldn't find you."

"Did you fight with Abe and Gav?" asked Meat, not one for the niceties.

Harper shot him a death glare, but he took it without bursting into flames and just sneered.

"I... It was the weirdest thing," whispered Stu, his voice sounding as if he was far away. He shook out his lank hair, a sheen of sweat on his tanned face, and smiled weakly at Harper. Then he seemed to realise what was happening as he looked down at his hand and then at us gathered around in a tight group to hear his quiet words.

"What was, love?" asked Harper.

"I just wanted a walk, and I remembered the bridge, so was strolling along happily. I'd been to visit Abe and Gav, clear the air kind of thing as you know we had a run-in, and they were both cool. Gav forgave me for losing my temper with him, but it was no big deal anyway, and I nabbed a slice of cheese from the counter then came for my walk. But then I felt weird, so had a sit, and I guess I've been here ever since."

"You took some cheese from the motorhome?" shrieked Harper.

"Yes, so what? It was only a tiny crumb, nothing much. I didn't even enjoy it really, and I know you've been on at me to watch my weight."

"Oh, Stu, you're perfect the way you are," sobbed Harper, flinging her arms around him and hugging the startled man tight.

"Well, that's good to hear. And did you all really come to find me? I wasn't gone long, was I?"

"Quite a while, mate, and things have been intense while you've been out here," said Ronnie, exchanging a look with me, both of us knowing this was far from right.

"You need to see a doctor," said Tanya.

"No, I'm fine," said Stu. "What's this about? Can't a bloke go for a walk?"

"Yes, of course, but tell us what happened?" said Harper. "How did you feel?"

"I was light-headed, then I felt sick, and then my heart started pounding. Like super fast. I thought I was having a heart attack for a moment, so like I said I sat down here. My heart slowed, but I still felt sick. I couldn't focus or anything, and I guess I lost track of time. Is it lunch time yet?" he asked hopefully.

"No lunch for you," said Harper. "We need to get you to the hospital."

"I told you, it was nothing. Probably just the upset and you being cross with me and everyone thinking I had something to do with it because I had a few words with Dexter and the guys in the band."

"What was it about?" I asked.

"Nothing much. Just over food with Dexter. And a little misunderstanding with the lads. I heard them joking about, saying we were past it for wanting to dance. They should know better. It wasn't very nice, so I guess I waded in being fierce. But we sorted it, like I told you." Stu shrugged; it was clearly no big deal to him.

"Well, mister, Abe is dead, Gav's been taken to the hospital after nearly dying, and it seems you're lucky to be alive. How'd you like them eggs?" Harper stood, hands on hips, and added, "We're going to the hospital."

"Abe's dead? But I just saw him. Damn, I'm hot. Is anyone else hot?" Stu wore shorts and a faded vest, but he was red and sweating. "My heart's going like the clappers again."

"Come on, let's get you back to the pub. I'll drive you to the hospital. An ambulance might take too long," said Ronnie.

"I'm fine. Heartburn or something." Stu stood, and his colour did return to normal, but he wasn't too steady on his feet.

"Someone poisoned them, Stu," said Harper. "And you got off lightly. It must have been the cheese, and you tasted it. Obviously not enough to kill you, but it's still in your system. You need to see someone."

"Okay, love, if you insist. Maybe you're right."

Ronnie and Meat stepped to either side of Stu and basically carried him back to the pub. He complained the whole way about being able to walk, but his feet hardly touched the ground and Harper told him repeatedly to behave until he relented and let them help him.

Back at the pub, Ronnie grabbed a few things and left with Harper and Stu, leaving us to deal with the police and numerous teams like earlier, the whole sorry process being repeated all over again. He returned soon enough, and joined us after explaining that Stu had been taken straight in for tests and Harper was with him.

We gathered on the grass, staying out of the way, while they went about the business of photographing everything, cataloguing endless items, and once the detectives had spent an inordinate amount of time inside the motorhome, poor Abe was taken away and the place was checked over with even more police and I assumed in even more detail. Endless bags of evidence were removed, specialists dealt with the high risk of poison being present, and as yet more people arrived and more work was carried out, DC Dolores came to speak to us properly having only spared the time for a quick update on what had happened until now.

With everyone firing off questions at the same time, she asked for calm then we explained what had happened. She confirmed it was what she'd already heard from the officers who had taken our statements, and that for now we weren't needed for anything else.

Ronnie was panicked about the whole site becoming a no-go zone, but she reassured him that the matter was being dealt with. He most certainly wasn't allowed to open, though, and no new campervans or tents were to be allowed on site. Ronnie went off in a huff, followed by Meat and Tanya, leaving Min and me with Dolores.

"Any developments since last night?" I asked.

"Nothing. The specialists are testing for poisons, but unless you know what you're looking for, it can be a lengthy process, apparently. I have zero experience of poison, and it's not exactly a common thing in the UK. Who does that?"

"A maniac?" I said.

"Yeah, a right nut job." Dolores sighed and rubbed at her pale skin, then frowned. "Sorry, that wasn't very professional, but this is one of those cases that gets under your skin. I've got more suspects than I know what to do with, no reason to actually take anyone in for questioning as it seems everyone has an alibi of some description, but these things could have been done at any time and people can always slip away for a few minutes."

"What's your gut instinct?" asked Min.

"That this is personal."

"That's what I think too," I agreed.

"Why do you both say that? Surely nobody has this much of a grudge against so many people," said Min.

"That's what I'm trying to find out. It would help if we knew how it was done. What was used and when. You guys were out all morning, right?"

"Yes, in the village learning about this crazy 1107 thing and it being fifty years soon that they've kept the same numbers."

"And they're pretty excited, right? I don't get it, but the locals rave about how this place is special and have been getting antsy this year about the numbers being wrong."

"It is an odd thing," I agreed.

"Did you see anything strange when you returned? And I assume your folks left before today's madness kicked off?"

"They did. We ate too much food, all bought from the village, but thinking about it now makes me queasy."

"We could have been poisoned too," said Min with a shudder.

"Maybe, but I don't think so. Everyone who has been killed is from the area. The band live in Boar and would have been off home later. Dexter lived on the premises here. Stu wasn't a target, he just happened to be in the wrong place at the wrong time."

"You've spoken to everyone, right?" I asked.

"Everyone I can think of. The stallholders were questioned, now they're home, too, but I'll check on them later, and that odd guy, Barry, told me he was leaving, but he didn't seem the type to do something like this."

"I still need to speak to him," I grumbled. "I can't believe he really was spying on me. I've been seeing him everywhere ever since I started this new life, and he always denied following me. Now I find out he's a private detective, and I want to know what the deal is."

"Then go chat to him. He's literally a mile away the other side of the river. At a small campsite."

"He is?"

"Yes, and he better stay there until this is over. That goes for you two as well. No leaving the area until this is solved or I'm happy everyone is safe."

"We have to stay here?" asked Min, tugging at my arm.

"No, but stay close. I understand if you need to leave for work, Mrs. Effort, but I want to know about it first, okay?"

"Sure, but I'm staying until I know Max is safe."

"You should go," I told Min. "It's beyond dangerous here now."

"No, I'm staying, and I will not discuss this again."

I failed to hold back a smile and said, "Some things never change. You've always had a stubborn streak."

"That's rich coming from you," laughed Min, slapping at my arm.

"Yes, well, I can see you're both very amused by this, so I'll leave you to it." Dolores spun on her heels then turned back and said, "You know this is extremely dangerous, don't you?"

"We do. Sorry to act like we aren't taking this seriously, because we are. It's just how we are around each other sometimes. Dolores, I have the feeling everything's coming together, and we're overlooking something vital. Does that make sense?"

"Yes, and I feel the same, Max. You definitely chose the wrong profession. From all I've heard about you, and from what I've seen, then I know you would have made a fine detective."

"Thank you. That means a lot. So it's okay for us to keep trying to figure this out?"

"Like I told you before. As long as you don't get in our way, I'm good with that. But watch your backs, and please don't eat any cheese you find lying about." Dolores nodded to us both then returned to the motorhome and the posse of officialdom gathered outside.

"Let's put this thing with Barry to bed once and for all," I said to Min. "It's something to do. It'll get us away from here for a while, and hopefully it will be calmer when we return."

"Good idea. I'll get the baseball bat, you get the sawn-off shotgun." Min pretend-cocked a gun and looked down the scopes.

"You don't get scopes with a sawn-off," I tutted.

"You do with mine. It's special."

Pretend weapon slung over her shoulder, we marched to the camper, sorted out a few things, called for Anxious, then headed for the final showdown with Volvo Barry.

Chapter 16

We found the campsite after a quick online search, and arrived to find that it was very quiet, just a few pitches taken. Barry was in a corner, sitting on a camping chair but without his tent assembled.

"What's his game?" I asked as we crossed the neatly mown field.

"Maybe he changed his mind and isn't staying."

"Or maybe he's waiting until he sees what I end up doing. Then he can follow me if I leave. I'm getting so paranoid I wouldn't put it past him to have put a tracker in Vee."

"Now that really is paranoid," laughed Min.

We paused in the middle of the field and turned to each other.

"Do you think it could be him?" we both asked, then chuckled as we said, "Jinx!"

"Not really," I admitted.

"Me either. He's odd, but he isn't a killer. Come on, time for answers."

The moment Barry noticed us coming, he jumped from his chair and rushed to his Volvo, flung open a back door, and began pulling out camping gear. It was too little, too late, and utterly unconvincing. He was not planning on setting up camp unless he had to, and that was down to me and what I would do. I was certain of that now.

"Barry, enough with the games, okay?" I sighed as we stopped beside the brown car, shaking our heads at the man dressed in brown like he was trying to blend in with the drab vehicle.

"Fine," he sighed, dumping his sleeping bag back inside. "I'm surprised you came looking for me."

"And I'm surprised you left when you could have kept an eye on me from the pub."

"You know who I am now, and I didn't want to talk to you. Plus, I didn't want to get poisoned. You're a dangerous man to be around."

"Me? Why?"

"Because everyone keeps dying. It's rather stressful." Barry ran a thin hand through his greasy hair before meeting my gaze and adding, "I'm not paid enough for this. Camping, and the heat, and having to buy all this equipment. I expected it to be a quick job."

"And what is the job?" asked Min. "Why are you so intent on following Max?"

"Let's sit down and I'll explain. I suppose it's time." Barry indicated the single cheap camping chair then realised his mistake and pulled out a blanket.

"Min, you take the chair," I suggested.

"Thanks."

Once we were seated, it feeling utterly incongruous and like we were about to have a nice picnic, Barry began without any more questions.

"I work for one of the best, and I do mean best, restaurants in the country, Max. They heard about you leaving your last place and they were interested. Very interested."

"I got offers all the time," I shrugged.

"Yes, but these people are more than keen. I've never known anything like it, but they were absolutely not going to take no for an answer."

"But they didn't reach out to me?" I asked, perplexed.

"No, they didn't, because they know about your new life and it was only once you'd left that they finally decided they needed you."

"That's weird," said Min.

Anxious took a tentative lick of Barry's corduroys, coughed, then scooted over to me and lay down by my leg, eyeing up the trousers, and Barry, with suspicion. Maybe he tasted wrong.

"What I mean is, they were waiting for you to be ready to return to work, give you some time, thinking once you got back in the business they could poach you. But then you upped and left and they called me in, made me an offer I couldn't refuse, and I chased after you."

"You came the day they got in touch?" I asked.

"If you knew who it was, then you wouldn't be surprised. You don't say no to these guys. I'm no camper."

"And no bird watcher either," I hissed.

"Yes, sorry about that, but I didn't know what to say. Anyway, I came, I watched, I reported back, and they kept telling me to stick with you and they'd inform me when the time was right."

"Right for what, Barry? I'm not liking the sound of this."

Anxious whined and put his paws over his head like he didn't want to hear the rest, but how bad could it be?

"For when I could swoop in and make you an offer that you would have to take."

"That's not going to happen."

"I told them that. I said that you seemed perfectly happy with your decision, and that there was no way to make you return to being a chef, but they insisted I stay watching you and waiting."

"For?" I pressed.

"For it to go wrong, which it has multiple times, and I assumed you'd go back home, but you didn't. I gave my reports, said you were a nice guy, seemed to have a real knack for uncovering the murders that kept happening, and that you weren't looking like you were going to go racing back home and call it quits."

"Um, thanks, I think. What did they say?"

"Just stick with it, and wait. That it would happen. I called them after the poisoning, and they said to clear out and then once everything settled to make you the offer. In fact, they just heard, and so did I, about what happened earlier. They think you'll definitely agree to it now."

"Why would I?"

"Because you'd realise it was too dangerous to be travelling. That you weren't cut out for it. Max, I told them I didn't think that was the case, but they insisted. I was going to come and find you later once the dust settled and pass on the offer. I'm sorry about spying on you, and to be honest I did a terrible job of it."

"You really did. How come you kept being spotted? Aren't private investigators meant to be excellent at stakeouts?"

"In the movies, maybe, but the reality is that most of my work is day-to-day stuff. Research, the odd stakeout, yes, but not trying to follow people around the country. I know what I am, and I'm a jobbing investigator who snaps a few photos of cheating husbands or finds out where a businessman might have been moonlighting for another company, that kind of thing. Regular stuff. This has been weird from day one, and I'm glad it's over."

"So, what's the offer?" asked Min, eyes gleaming.

"I don't want to hear it," I insisted. "Come on, we're going." I stood, and Anxious stretched and yawned then joined me, but Min remained seated.

"What's the offer, Barry?" She fixed first him, then me, with a hard glare. "Max, you need to hear it. You say you've changed, you say the new you is done with that life. Well, now's your chance to prove it. Hear what the offer is, think about it, then decide."

"I don't need to know. Min, you said you don't always trust me, but now here's your chance, not mine. I don't want the job. I will never return to that life."

"It's a million pounds a year, a massive house with a swimming pool in your name, a car of your choice, and you sign a contract to promise you won't work for anyone else or quit for five years then you can be done forever and you'll be astonishingly rich. In five years you'll be thirty-eight and you and your family, if you have one," he coughed nervously as he looked to Min, "will never have to think about money again. If you have children, they'll be set for life, Max. It's an incredible offer, quite amazing in fact, and you're one lucky guy."

"Done," I agreed.

"Really?" asked Barry, sighing with relief.

"No, not done! Of course not! I don't want the job."

"But it's so much money. People would kill for cash like that. A future like that. Think about your legacy. About having a family and what you could do for them."

Ignoring Barry, I turned to Min and sank to my knees. Anxious happily came over beside me and sat. I took her hands as her moist eyes met mine. Not wanting to be left out, Anxious stood on his hind legs and placed a paw over mine.

"It doesn't matter how much money they offer me. Nice houses, fancy cars, any of it. I'm never returning to that life. I promise. Whether we eventually make this right between us, or just stay friends, I will not go back."

"Not even for all that money? You could work a few years then relax forever."

"No, Min, I couldn't. I've already ruined so much, and if I spend five years in a kitchen I won't emerge as the man I want to be. And where will you be then? I'd hardly see you, hardly see Anxious, and miss out on too much. I promised you, remember? But I also promised myself. I'm done with that. All of it."

"That's very commendable," came a loud voice I didn't recognise.

Anxious growled as he turned to confront the intruder, but there was nobody there, just Barry holding up his phone.

"It's on loudspeaker," he said, shaking his head to say he was sorry.

"Who's speaking?" I asked.

The man gave his name and the restaurant they wanted me to work at, and I couldn't believe it. It was every top chef's dream job, and I knew Barry wasn't lying about the wages or the perks. They could afford it and then some.

"Max, you should take it," said Min with tears in her eyes.

"Listen to her, Max. I know you've been through some things, but it can be different this time. I've had regular reports about how you've been doing, and I think you're ready to jump back into things. Barry doesn't think so, but I know chefs, and I know you. You miss it, don't you?"

"I do, but not as much as I miss my ex-wife. Not as much as I miss being the man I should have always been. Thank you for the offer, but it's a no. I'm happy, do you understand that? Happy to be out here, happy to have a new, meaningful calling. Helping people. I won't ever return to my old ways. But thank you. Now, call off your spy and go find someone else."

I reached out and jabbed the end call button.

"You're crazy," said Barry, shaking his head. "But I admire you. Sorry to have been so duplicitous, but it was work, you understand?"

"I understand. Now we're done?"

"Yes, I imagine so. I'll call them back in a while and clear everything up, but yes, I suppose my business with you is over."

"You meant it, didn't you?" gushed Min, flinging herself at me and wrapping her arms around my waist, her face buried in my T-shirt.

"Of course I did. Just cooking in the pub made me realise I could never do that kind of work again, and I have enough money to keep me going as long as I don't get extravagant. Min, I know you'd like a swimming pool and a large house, but I'm sorry, I won't do it."

Min tensed, then relaxed, but pushed away from me and said, "All I ever wanted was my husband," then stormed off across the field.

"Bugger. Wait here, Barry, we still need to talk." I chased after Min and caught her up. "Sorry, that came out wrong. What I meant was that it would be nice, that of course everyone wants that. Not that you actually want me to do it."

"It just got too much. Max, I don't want you to give up on your dreams. It's a stunning offer and you should think about it. Don't turn it down because of me. I've told you, we might never get back together in the way you want. We need to wait and see what happens. You might miss out on this and for what?"

"Don't you get it? I know all that. I'd resigned myself to us never getting back together until I left for this mad new life. But either way, I'm done with that old life. I need something else, something real. Out here is real, not stuck inside and obsessing over purees and jus."

"You mean it, don't you? Truly?"

"Yes. With all my heart."

"I'm so proud of you!"

Min took my hand and we returned to Barry, who was looking rather confused by the whole business.

"So you're sure?" he asked. "I need to call them back and they'll want a proper explanation. What should I tell them?"

"Tell them I'm not interested because I have found a new passion, and an old one." I turned to Min and smiled. "But not very old. Um, you know what I meant," I sighed, the words coming out all wrong.

"Of course."

"Okay then. I guess I'll make the call. Before I do, can you explain what happened at the pub? Who exactly died, and what did the police say?"

"It was awful," said Min. "Abe, one of the members of the folk band, was dead in the motorhome. Gav came stumbling out and looked like he was next, but the paramedics got to him in time. Then we thought Stu was the culprit and couldn't find him, but he ate some tainted cheese and was most likely close to death for a while too. They poisoned the sandwiches."

"That's awful. So no closer to knowing who did it? Nothing from the police?"

"Not yet. It is early days. All this happened today and yesterday, but no, there's nothing."

"This whole area is just strange," said Barry. "I was in the village, Boar, earlier and it's rather fascinating, but quite odd. Have you heard about the fact that the number of residents has been the same for almost fifty years and they're planning a massive golden jubilee to celebrate? Everyone's been stressed about the numbers not being right though."

"We heard. It's beyond odd, right?"

"Absolutely. I heard there was a baby born, though, and another on the way soon." Barry thought for a moment, then said, "I suppose with three people dead, the numbers will work out as long as the baby is born before the deadline."

"I suppose it will now, yes. That will be one lucky baby," I said.

"It really will. Amazing for the child," beamed Barry.

"What do you mean?" asked Min. "You think it will bring it good luck?"

"Oh, I know it will." Barry clapped his hands together happily.

Min and I shrugged as we looked at each other, then Barry. "How do you mean? " I asked.

"Ever since the first year this happened, the entire village has been putting money into an account. Raffles, little events, things like that, they all offer something to the charity the village set up. It's very superstitious, but they did it from the first year, and every year when the numbers were right they added a little more. There's a fortune in it now. Think about it. Even if everyone in the village only gave a pound a year, over fifty years that's fifty thousand, but it's much more. With extra fundraisers, the festivals, fetes, and what have you, these old guys at the bowling green told me there's over two hundred grand in the pot now."

"Wow, that's a lot of money."

"It sure is. Gav's granddaughter will have a life very different from his and his daughter's."

"You lost me there," I admitted.

"Apparently, Gav has a wife and daughter. And his daughter is the one about to give birth. The youngest and oldest residents on the day of the fiftieth anniversary get the entire pot split equally between them. How about that?"

"We need to go," I told Min.

"What? Why?"

"Um, just something we have to do. I forgot. And Barry?"

"Yes?"

"I won't ever see you again, will I?"

"No, you won't."

"Good. No offence, and I understand you were just doing your job, but I hope you're right. Explain to your boss that I'm sincere and have a new calling. And that is solving murders and helping out those in need. Later."

I took Min's hand and raced back across the field.

"What's going on?" she whispered. "Why are you acting so weird?"

"We need to go and visit Gav in hospital. If he's out of intensive care."

"That's sweet, but why the urgency?"

"Min, didn't you hear what Barry just said? His granddaughter is about to inherit a fortune."

"Yes, so?"

"And that means he had a motive."

"Max, he's in the hospital. He ate a poisoned sandwich. The poor man nearly died."

"Did he? Or did he know exactly what he was doing and ate just enough to make it look like the mystery killer tried to murder him too?"

"You can't be serious?"

"Let me think this through, but yes, I am serious. Come on let's go."

Chapter 17

"Do you truly believe it was Gav who did this?" asked Min as I floored the accelerator and navigated the lanes leading from the campsite.

"It does make sense. He could have poisoned everyone but given himself just enough to get ill but nothing fatal."

"That's a big risk. What if he went too far and ended up dead himself?"

"Just let me take this turn and get onto the main road, then we can go over this, okay?"

Min fidgeted with Anxious who was on her lap while I checked for traffic and got Vee up to speed and headed for the hospital, then I took a deep breath and just let words come out without thinking about anything too much. Not quite stream of consciousness, but nothing mulled over too much either.

"If Gav's daughter is about to give birth, it's clearly a strong motive. With three people dead, that sets up his family for a big windfall. He might have just given himself a tiny amount of the poison, or even taken something else to become ill and just pretended he was worse than he seemed. It's a perfect alibi. It couldn't have been him because he was poisoned too. Pretty smart."

"It may be smart, but it's also dumb. If he did poison himself, it could have easily gone wrong. That's a massive risk to take."

"You know what they say. No risk, no reward."

"And where would he get the poison from?"

"Where would anyone? I'm not saying it definitely is him, and I haven't had the time to think this through properly, but you have to admit it's worth investigating. Maybe it isn't him, maybe there's something obvious we're missing, but we need to talk to him anyway. If nothing else, we can see how poorly he really is, and ask if he has any insights into what might have happened."

"Yes, that's a good idea." Min checked her phone after pulling up the directions to the hospital, and we spent the next twenty minutes navigating the convoluted road system until we found it.

"Why are there never enough parking spaces?" I lamented after driving around the car park for the third time.

"They don't want people coming and causing them lots of grief and getting in the way."

"That's dumb. If loved ones are in hospital, then of course they should be able to have visitors. Look, there's a spot!" I put on my indicator and pulled up alongside the rows of cars, then began to reverse. Still having done zero practice, it was not a pretty sight, and I ignored the chuckles of Min as I went back and forth trying to line up the campervan and get parked.

I managed it eventually, but I was flustered and wasn't even sure there was room to open the doors of the old camper.

"Well done, my hero!" Min clapped as she grinned at me. "You're a natural."

"No need to be sarcastic," I huffed, but took her ribbing in the spirit it was intended.

The heat was intense and building the moment I parked, so there was no way Anxious could remain in the van. We tied him up outside the entrance in the shade of the overhang with plenty of water in his bowl and a few treats so he wouldn't sulk, then went inside to ask at reception about Gav.

Although not strictly visiting hours, we were told we could go and see Gav and that he was in a private room as that was the norm for cases of suspected poisoning. Both of us were rather shocked to be granted access, but when we arrived at the ward and spoke to the staff nurse, she explained that Gav wasn't in any danger and it hadn't been a very serious case despite how bad he'd looked immediately after eating his lunch.

We still had to wear surgical masks and gloves as a precaution, and were instructed not to touch him and to keep our distance. As much for his safety as ours, as his immune system was compromised by the ordeal.

The room was rather dark with the blue curtains drawn halfway, the bitter antiseptic smell typical of all hospitals stronger than usual. Most likely he'd been thoroughly cleaned to ensure there was no poison residue on his hands, although I didn't know what the procedure might be. For them to have let us visit must have meant they weren't unduly concerned, but this still seemed odd to both me and Min as we shrugged and the door closed behind us.

"Hi, Gav. It's Max and Min from the VW. How are you feeling?"

Gav shifted in the bed where he was propped up on a mound of pillows and his eyes opened. He looked pale and his skin was waxy. His long hair was damp against his scalp and tucked behind large ears, his thick beard making him look the part of a folk musician.

"I'm not so bad. Yourselves?"

"We're good. Just concerned. What did the doctors say? What happened once you got here? We were surprised to be allowed in to see you so soon."

"I'm not sure they know what to do with me," he laughed weakly, then coughed.

"Your voice sounds raw. Is your throat hurting?" asked Min.

"Like you wouldn't believe. They put tubes down and made me vomit and gave me one helluva scrubbing too. But I'm alive. Luckier than everyone else who got poisoned."

"Why do you think you made it through?" I asked.

"I only had a bite of my sandwich. Abe has always been a fast eater so he gobbled his up. I wasn't in the mood for eating after all the stress, so he had most of mine too. I had a bite or two and that was it. The doctors reckon that it was still close, but if I made it through the first few minutes then I'd most likely be fine. And don't worry, being poisoned isn't contagious, so I'm good. It's not like they used slow release radioactive stuff or anything. Do you remember that poor Russian guy who took weeks to succumb? Ugh, can you imagine?"

Min and I shuddered at the thought. That would be a horrendous way to go.

"Have your wife and daughter visited?" I asked.

"Not a chance! I spoke to them on the phone, and warned them not to come. My daughter's due any day and there is no way I would risk her or the babies."

"Babies?" I asked, confused. "She's had another baby recently?"

"No, she's overdue, and expecting twins. We kept it quiet as Boar is terrible for gossip, but she'll have her hands full, that's for sure. Me and the missus will help out, though, and although it will be a struggle for the finances, my little girl has a good husband who earns decent wages so they'll be okay."

"We didn't know it was to be twins," said Min. We looked at each other knowingly; this changed everything.

"Why would you? Hardly anyone knows. Just close family, and the doctors and nurses, of course. Mind you, around here that most likely means just about everyone, as nobody seems to be able to keep their mouths shut."

"So you were meant to be killed," I mused, trying to get this straight in my head.

"Did you see what happened to me?" he spluttered. "Of course I was meant to be killed. What are you talking about?"

"It's this fifty-year celebration thing about the population of Boar. With you surviving, we thought the numbers had worked out, that your daughter stood to get half of the big payout as your grandchild would be the youngest. But if she's having twins, that means the killer really did want you dead."

"Yeah, that's a shame about the money. The family sure could use it, but it does look like we'll be one person too many. Maybe I should have croaked it. At least then I'd have gone out with a real purpose and my family would be taken care of."

"Don't talk like that, Gav," said Min softly. "You get to see your grandchildren grow, and that's priceless."

"I know, and I was only joking around. It's going to be amazing. I'll get the little ones a fiddle and they'll be playing before they can walk," he laughed, eyes sparkling as the light caught his face. "I'm a lucky guy and I know it. But I guess there's no more band. I still can't believe Abe and Carter are dead. We've been together for so long, and been to so many places. Now it's over. We had our issues, and I was even thinking of packing it all in and taking my wife back out to South America, but with the twins on the way I knew that wasn't going to happen."

"We're so sorry," I said.

"Yeah, well, maybe the oldest guy in Boar will croak it and then the numbers will be right and the next in line will get half and one of my grandchildren will get the other half. Matty, that's my daughter, has always joked that if the money did ever get given to one of the twins, she'd split it between them."

"That's sweet of her. I wonder who the oldest person is? Do you know?" asked Min.

"Sure, of course." Gav frowned, then his eyes went wide and he asked, "You are not serious? You don't think these poisonings are so someone can get half the golden jubilee money?"

"Yes, we do," I said. "And the fact your daughter is expecting twins means that as long as she gives birth when expected, there will still be too many people in Boar so nobody gets anything."

"Which means you were meant to die," said Min, nodding to me.

"It sure feels like they tried," said Gav. "But this is crazy talk. Nobody does things like that."

"People do all kinds of utterly mad things, Gav," I said, knowing from firsthand experience the depths people could sink to. "And with you being alive, it means that the killer hasn't finished yet. They need one more victim and then the golden jubilee can go ahead."

"Gav, one last question, then we'll leave you in peace," said Min.

"Yes?"

"Exactly who is the oldest person in Boar?"

Chapter 18

"Do you really think you've got it right this time?" asked Min as I pressed the accelerator to the floor, not that it made much difference.

"Do you?"

"We did just think it was Gav."

"Suspected. We suspected it was him, but went to ask a few questions to be sure. Now we'll do the same again. I'm not saying this is definite, but you have to admit it's highly likely. We should have seen this coming earlier. I should have. The more I think about it, the more obvious it is."

"Max, none of this is obvious. What on earth are you talking about?"

"Imagine how easy it would be to poison the pickles and kill Dexter then do the same to Carter. Nobody would blink an eye seeing our suspect coming and going. But it's not even that, it's other things. The truth was staring us in the face the whole time. Damn, why won't this thing go any faster?" I pressed harder on the pedal but our speed didn't increase.

"Maybe changing from second gear would help?" suggested Min with a raised eyebrow and a wicked smirk.

"No need to be smug," I grunted, then laughed, the tension easing. I shifted up into third, then fourth, and Vee put on a spurt of speed as I floored it again and we sped back towards the pub.

"Is your heart beating fast? Because mine is." Min took several deep breaths through her nose to calm herself.

"It's the excitement and the nerves. Yes, mine's going really fast, but not as fast as it will be in a few minutes. Can you call the DC and tell her to meet us at the pub? Tell her we think we know who did it, and she should probably bring backup."

"You think? What if you're wrong?"

"Not this time. Gav was a likely suspect, but this is a different kind of feeling. I'm sure."

"I don't get the same feelings like you do. No tingle, no certainty, but the logical thing is that yes, you're right. What else makes you sure we have the right person?"

"Let's just speak to the detective and ensure she's coming, then we can talk about it, okay?"

Min nodded, then made the call. There was no answer so she left a message, but the moment she hung up DC Dolores returned the call. Min explained what we'd been doing, what our suspicions were, and that she should come to the pub with the means to make the arrest. Although dubious, Dolores agreed to meet us there as soon as she possibly could.

By the time the conversation was over, I was pulling up beside my sun shelter. It felt very strange to see it and my kitchen setup, the camping chairs, and the motorhomes like nothing awful had happened here at The Dead Crow, but people were dead, there was a murderer on the loose, and, seemingly, we were the only ones who had put the pieces together.

We sat for a moment, trying to calm down, then both turned as we heard Stu and Harper's motorhome start up then reverse.

"We have to stop them!" I shouted, then hurried out with Min and Anxious on my heels.

As the motorhome crawled forward, I jumped in front of it, waving my arms and shouting, "Wait!"

Harper stopped and I heard the handbrake click on, then she killed the engine. I ran over to the driver's side and checked Stu was with her. He was.

"What on earth are you doing?" asked Harper.

"You're leaving? Were you coming back?"

"No, we're off. This place is a deathtrap. I'm getting Stu out of here."

"Why are you here?" I asked Stu. "Shouldn't you be in the hospital?"

They exchanged a guilty look and Stu admitted, "We snuck out. They wanted to keep me in for observation, but I'm not sitting around in a hospital waiting to be killed next. Harper thought it best if we just go."

"That's right," she said defensively, glaring at me and daring me to argue.

"Okay, well, that's up to you guys. But I want everyone to come into the pub. Can you do that? Spare us a few minutes?"

"What's all this about, Max? And, Min, are you in on this?"

"Yes, and please can you come inside so we can explain? Actually, Max will explain, as he knows what's going on better than I do."

"Let's just go," said Stu. "I've had more than enough of this place."

"Sorry to leave without saying goodbye, but we don't want to stay here any longer," said Harper. "It's been great to meet you, but we're out of here."

"I know who the killer is," I blurted.

"Don't care. We're going," snapped Harper.

She moved to start the engine, but Stu put a hand over hers and said, "Not until we hear them out. This has gone on long enough and too many people have died. If he thinks he knows, then I want to hear what Max has to say."

Harper sighed, then her shoulders relaxed. She smiled at Stu then turned and said, "Fine, but I'm not happy about this. If anything happens, it's on you two."

I nodded, relieved when they exited the motorhome and joined us.

Anxious wagged happily and rubbed against Stu until he got a fuss. It seemed to cheer Stu up and he laughed as Anxious ran over to the pub then sat, head cocked, waiting for us.

"He's such a cute dog," said Stu.

"And he likes you. I'm glad you're okay, Stu. I thought you were in real trouble earlier."

"Nah, just felt dodgy for a while, but I'm good. The doctors won't be happy, but I'm better off out here than in the hospital."

"He is, and we want to get away from this place," said Harper.

"Just a few minutes, then you can go if you want to. Everything will be revealed."

"Oh, how exciting!" Stu clapped his hands and grinned at me. "The amateur sleuth is doing his thing."

"It isn't like that," I mumbled.

"Max, it totally is," laughed Min.

Anxious barked from the pub door.

I squared my shoulders, nodded to everyone, then led the way.

Ronnie had clearly got fed up with the crime scene tape so had ripped it off, leaving a ragged little strip behind. I pushed on the doors and entered the gloomy interior, pleased to be out of the heat.

"Ronnie," I called out. I turned as I heard the door bang shut, noting Min ushering Stu and Harper inside. Anxious already had his spot next to me, sitting and waiting for things to unfold.

"I'm in here," Ronnie called from the back.

"Where are you?" I shouted.

"In the kitchen. Stop shouting!" he hollered.

Ronnie, Meat, and Tanya came down the hallway and into the pub. Tanya took up her usual spot behind the bar whilst Ronnie and Meat joined us.

"No, don't eat that!" I hissed, racing forward and slapping a shop bought sandwich from his hand. The cardboard wrapping and cellophane remained clutched tight as half the tuna mayonnaise sandwich slapped onto the flagstones.

"What the hell? I was just about to eat that."

"I know. But don't. Meat, have you eaten anything yet?"

"Um, no. It's still in the wrapper, see?" He lifted his hand to show his packaged sandwich.

"Good, great. That's a relief."

"Max, what's got into you? I know everyone's paranoid about the poisoning, but we've been careful. Um, I thought you guys were off?" he asked Stu and Harper.

"We were, but Max dragged us back inside," said Stu, frowning at the mess on the floor.

"Anxious, do not eat that," I warned, then decided it wasn't worth the risk and raced into the back leaving everyone there, grabbed a dustpan and brush, hurried back, then cleaned up the mess and for good measure grabbed a cardboard box, flattened it, and placed it over the sticky remains. "There, that should stop him. Good boy."

Anxious wagged happily, having not moved a muscle.

"Have you lost your mind?" asked Ronnie.

"No, I haven't. Tanya, have you eaten anything?"

"Not yet. I was about to, but now you're freaking me out." She brushed her long hair from her face as she frowned. Her dark eyes focused on mine, shrouded with thick eye-liner, but when I held her gaze I could see she knew and her mouth opened as her eyes widened and she gasped.

Everyone focused on her and she coughed to clear her throat, then said, "I gotta go. Things to do."

"Not yet, you don't," I said. "You stay right there. I called the police. They'll be here soon."

"Okay," she said warily, her frown deepening. "But I still gotta go."

"No."

"Max, I don't know what's going on, and you've been a great guy so far, but that's no way to speak to her. Watch your tone," growled Ronnie.

"Yeah, she's family. You speak nice to her," said Meat.

"I wasn't being rude. Okay, maybe a little, but for good reason. Ronnie, where'd the food come from?"

"Tanya nipped out to get it for us. The police said not to risk anything from around here, so she popped to the shops and got us some grub. It's not a proper dinner, but it will do for today."

"But you haven't eaten it yet?" I asked again, just to be sure.

"No, like I just said."

"We just went to visit Gav," I said.

"How's he doing?"

"Good. He'll make it. You know, I thought it was him. That he'd given himself a mild dose of poison to avoid suspicion. It would have been the perfect crime."

"Why would he do that?" asked Ronnie.

"Because we learned about the golden jubilee money and figured with three people dead his daughter's baby would get half of the money on offer."

"I guess that's a pretty good motive. Hadn't thought of that. Problem being, she's expecting twins."

"That's what we just found out. Which means the killer tried to poison him for real and wanted him dead. But now it means there will be one too many people left alive and nobody will get the prize. Right Tanya?"

Tanya's head shot up as everyone turned to her, but she said nothing.

"What does he mean?" Ronnie asked her. "Tanya, is there something I should know?" Ronnie thought for a moment, then something clicked and he said, "Of course. Your grandad stands to get half the prize, doesn't he?"

"So what?" snapped Tanya, fidgeting with a tea towel and averting her gaze.

"It's motive," I said. "If the number of residents is right, then your grandad gets a lot of money and you're next in line, right?"

"Again, so what if I am? That doesn't mean I'm gonna go around killing people and trying to get the numbers right."

"I think it does," I insisted.

"Max, you can't be serious?" stammered Stu. "Tanya's a great gal, and would never do that. She's been working here for years."

"Let Max do his thing, love," said Harper. "Max, for a minute there I thought you were going to say it was me and I tried to murder my Stu."

"It crossed my mind," I said with a wink and a smile.

Harper laughed despite the seriousness of the situation.

"Max, that's enough!" shouted Ronnie. "Tanya is like family to us all here. We live together, work together, and play together."

"And that's the problem, right, Tanya? I never thought much of it, but that bruise on your arm you said you got when you tripped wasn't an accident, was it?"

Tanya rubbed at the faded purple and yellow mark on her bare upper arm and said, "I told you, I fell."

"No, I don't think you did. I think that Dexter was harassing you, and maybe it had been going on for a while. You discovered a way to get rid of him, then you must have figured if you were going to kill one person, you might as well kill four and then you'd stand to inherit the money once your granddad died. Not all the money, as obviously Gav's grandchildren would get the other half, but maybe that was enough to salve your conscience, the fact that his family would be taken care of."

"Did Dexter hurt you?" asked Meat softly. "He was always a little lewd, but he never touched you, did he?"

"He tried to," blurted Tanya, then her hand shot to her mouth.

"I'd bloody kill him if he wasn't dead," hissed Ronnie. "What did he do to you?"

"Nothing. It was nothing. Look, I have to go," Tanya pleaded, arms outstretched to Ronnie. "I need to go. This is too much and I can't think straight. All these accusations. How could you think that, Ronnie?"

"I didn't accuse you of nothin'! That was Max." Ronnie spun to me, arm raised, and pointed at the door. "Out! Go on, get out of my pub."

"Give me one minute and I'll prove it. One minute."

"Make this quick," growled Ronnie.

I retrieved the pack of sandwiches from the table and peeled back the cellophane, revealing the remaining sandwich that hadn't hit the floor. I took Meat's as well and placed both on the bar. "Prove you're innocent. You picked up the sandwiches from a shop and they haven't been out of your sight since. So take two bites from each. I don't know if you wanted to kill Ronnie or Meat, so you need to eat both. If you're innocent, then you know these are untainted."

"That was a good idea," whispered Stu to Harper.

"It was," she agreed.

"Well?"

"I'm not playing your dumb game, Max." Tanya folded her arms across her chest and pouted.

"Eat the sandwich, Tanya," ordered Ronnie as he and Meat stepped up to the bar. Everyone crowded around, not wanting their view blocked.

"I won't!"

"Do it. Max is out of order, but here's your way to prove you're innocent. Eat the damn sandwiches!"

Tanya's hand moved forward slowly, then she sighed and stepped back. "It was me, okay? I did it!"

"How could you?" demanded Ronnie.

"Dexter made my life a misery and you did nothing. You know what that fat slob was like and you let it happen."

"He just fooled around. He never laid a hand on you, did he?"

"Of course he did, that disgusting oaf. He hurt me the other day, and I'd had enough. I was talking to Gav about getting away and he started going on about South America yet again when he came for a pint and it got me to thinking."

"How did that get you to thinking?"

"The frogs, right?" I asked.

"The frogs," she agreed.

"Frogs?" asked Meat.

"Will everyone stop saying frogs?" hollered Ronnie.

"I had to get rid of Dexter. It was too much. And then I thought about the money I could have if four people died instead of just one. Carter was a creep, too, always getting handsy, and Gav was a good guy but I would have been doing him a favour. Setting up his grandchildren for life."

"What about Abe?" I asked.

Tanya shrugged. "I had to make up the numbers, and it seemed easier to poison both of them in their motorhome than just one. When Stu vanished, I figured I'd blown it and too many people would die, but then he was alright. But so was Gav, and now it was all for nothing. But at least I got rid of Dexter. And I'm not sorry about that."

"You would have killed me or Meat?" asked Ronnie, voice hoarse.

"You, Ronnie." Tanya locked eyes with him and didn't look away.

"Why? I thought of you like a sister. A little sister I looked out for."

"You did a very poor job of it. You didn't see, or didn't care, what was going on right under your own roof. This was your watch, Ronnie, and you didn't look out for me. So, yes, if you ate your sandwich you would have been next."

Ronnie lunged across the bar, but Tanya grabbed a bottle of vodka and smashed it over his head. His forehead slammed into the bar as spirits soaked Meat beside him, but Ronnie shook it off and lifted his head for a moment. Blood poured from his temple as his legs buckled and he keeled over.

"You ruined everything!" Tanya screamed as she flung a bottle of Glenfiddich at me. I ducked and it smashed to the floor.

"You killed them, Tanya. You killed innocent people. You'd have been found out."

"Not all of them were innocent. But I had no choice. I had to get out of this dump. Get away. Start again. It was Ronnie's fault. He said he'd protect me and he didn't."

Meat helped Ronnie to stand, and with the blood pouring from his head ignored, he said, "I'm sorry, Tanya, I truly am. Maybe I knew something wasn't right deep down, but chose not to think about it. I'm sorry."

"It's too late for that. That man was always making fun of me, being lewd, and the time he grabbed me was one time too many. I had to do it, don't you see?"

"You killed people, Tanya. That's a step too far."

"Look who's talking. The big tough gangster from London."

"You know that's an act. We didn't kill people. We might have roughed them up, but murder? And never innocents. You don't kill innocent people."

"Then you should have looked after me."

A wicked smile crossed Tanya's face as she pulled out a Zippo, flicked the lid, then struck the wheel. The flame burst into life first time and she just flung it at the bar. The spirits caught instantly, a whoosh forcing everyone to jump back.

Meat rushed to the door, grabbed the fire extinguisher, and quickly doused the flames, revealing Tanya had vanished.

"Where'd she go?" asked Ronnie, rubbing at his temple then inspecting his hand covered in blood. He shrugged, seemingly unconcerned, then rushed into the back. Meat was right behind him.

"Let's go out the front," I told the others, and we dashed out to stop Tanya before she escaped.

Chapter 19

We heard shouting from the car park and raced around the side to find Ronnie waving his arms and shouting as Tanya kick-started her motorbike. She yanked her helmet onto her head, revved the throttle, then sped right for him. Ronnie dove out of the way and Tanya skidded as she took the turn onto the lane, then brakes squealed as a police car and a white Subaru drove towards her. She righted, then sped past them and out of sight.

"Go after her," yelled Ronnie as he raced back towards the pub. "I'm gonna get my keys."

Dolores jumped from the Subaru and shouted, "What's going on?"

"No time, but it's Tanya. She killed everyone, and she's trying to get away. We need to go after her."

"Okay, but don't do anything stupid. We'll beat you to her anyway."

Min, Anxious, and I dashed over to Vee and buckled up then gave chase with Stu and Harper right behind us. A quick glance in the rearview showed Ronnie and Meat behind them in his classic Ford Escort and the two police vehicles catching up fast.

Our convoy sped along the country lane after Tanya, but it was obvious we didn't have a hope of catching her up until we hit the familiar roadworks and I grinned.

"There she is. Look, there's a truck coming and she can't get past."

"We're going to catch her. Should I just get out and try to grab her?" asked Min, face flushed, eyes sparkling.

"That might be dangerous. She killed people, remember?"

"There's nothing to her. She's only tiny. I can take her."

"Min, she's deranged. Just let the police deal with it. Look, the officers are after her now."

As I spoke, two police officers followed by Dolores ran past the camper and toward Tanya. She must have seen them, though, and the moment the truck was past she sped off, kicking up loose gravel even as another car approached through the temporary one-way system.

Min put her hands over her eyes and groaned, "I can't look," but I kept watching, gasping as Tanya just about made it between the car and the hedge.

The lights changed to green and I drove past the officers and DC who were rushing back to their vehicles.

With rapid gear changes, I managed to get up to fourth in record time, but it was no use and we were holding up the rest. The road widened and first Harper, then Ronnie, then the police all overtook us, leaving us to chase from behind.

I followed as fast as I could, and realised we were heading straight for Boar. Maybe Tanya was planning to grab some things from home before hightailing it out of here, but it would do her no good as there was no way she'd have time.

Traffic was light, but a few vehicles passed in the opposite direction, horns blaring, so Tanya was obviously driving dangerously and risking her life, but what could we do but try to stop her?

We caught up with the other vehicles a minute later and waited at a junction that led directly to the centre of the village and bowling green. The moment the traffic was clear, Tanya revved and was away, but she had been playing a dangerous game and another car came hurtling across the junction. Tanya tried to outmanoeuvre the car, but the back wheel kicked out and she skidded.

Incredibly, she managed to right herself but with a serious wobble, and then she was out of control and careening towards a wall. With incredible luck, she managed to hit the exact spot that gave entry to the bowling green. The motorbike nicked the side of the wall, she wobbled again, then bumped over the ditch, hopped up onto the pristine grass, hit a collection of bowls the two old-timers were walking towards to collect, gouged a massive groove in the grass, and slid sideways then fell off her bike. It dug into the ground then flipped over once and slid along the smooth, flat surface.

The men watched in utter astonishment then removed their caps and scratched liver-spotted heads as they hobbled towards Tanya.

I parked, and we ran to join the others converging on Tanya who was already on her feet.

"She's the pickled onion poisoner," shouted Ronnie as he stormed forward with Meat.

"Spread out," said Dolores to the two officers.

She took the middle, they took either side, Stu and Harper followed Dolores, and Min, Anxious, and I just rushed forward, not sure what to do but knowing we had to stop her.

Tanya spun, looking for an escape route, then laughed, wild and dangerous, as she spied what she thought was an easy way out. Directly between the approaching pensioners.

She ran straight at them, head down, aiming to bowl them over, but the wily old guys split apart, turned to each other, nodded, then as Tanya passed between them they just dove at her feet.

In a tangled heap, Tanya tripped over the men and slammed into the ground. They crawled over and sat on her back, grinning, as everyone converged on what was an utterly surreal scene.

Anxious raced ahead, jumped onto Tanya, and sat between the men, tail wagging as if he'd been the one to catch the killer.

"Thanks for the help," said Dolores as she nodded to the two officers and they secured Tanya in handcuffs then helped the men to stand. They hauled Tanya to her feet and removed her helmet.

She was wild-eyed and red-faced, but there was nowhere for her to go, nothing she could do, and her shoulders slumped in resignation.

"I don't suppose someone would like to tell me what's been going on here?" asked Dolores, locking eyes on me.

"Max said it was Tanya that killed everyone," said Ronnie. "I didn't believe him at first, but then she admitted it."

Everyone piped up, agreeing that they'd heard Tanya confess.

"But I know your grandad," said one of the old guys, scowling as he looked at his beloved bowling green.

"Me too. And look at the state of the green. How could you? And what's going on here? Little Tanya is no killer."

"I'm afraid she is," said Min. "She poisoned the pickled onions at the pub and the cheese sandwiches. She was after the golden jubilee money."

"You never did?" asked both men simultaneously.

"She did," I confirmed. "Everything made sense once we discovered that her grandfather is the oldest man in Boar. If the golden jubilee goes ahead, he's set to inherit half the money."

"That's the motive?" whistled Dolores. "I never even gave the money a thought. I'd heard the numbers were off this year anyway?"

"They were, but we found out that Gav's daughter is expecting twins, so if he'd died, the numbers would have been right and the payout given," I said.

"And there's more," said Harper.

"Yes, go on, Ronnie, tell them," said Stu, not wanting to be left out.

"It's not your fault, mate," said Meat. "I'm as much to blame as you."

"You're both to blame," spat Tanya, glaring at them.

"Someone better explain," sighed Dolores, rubbing at her face.

"Dexter, the chef, had been causing trouble for Tanya, but we thought it was just the usual banter. Seems he went too far and hurt her. She decided to take her revenge, but figured why not kill three more and get the payout?" said Ronnie, shaking his head.

"You're a bad un," said an old guy.

"Rotten apple," agreed the other. "Whose going to fix our bowling green? Took us years and years to get it this flat and this good, and now it's ruined. What are we meant to do now?"

"Sorry about the green," said Tanya. "But when grandad receives the money, I'll make sure he gets it fixed."

"But there is no payout now, Tanya," I said. "Remember, you didn't kill anyone else, so there's one person too many in Boar."

"We'll see. These things have a way of working out in the end," she said smugly.

"So you admit it?" asked Dolores.

"Not much point saying no now, is there?" she shrugged.

"Max, and everyone else, thank you. You did a great job figuring this out, although I would have appreciated a heads-up."

"Sorry, but it happened so fast. And we did call to tell you what was going on. We just got there first, and Tanya went nuts."

"I did not!"

"You smashed a bottle of vodka over my head!" said Ronnie, rubbing at the deep gash and wincing.

Tanya just grinned, but said nothing.

"So how did you do it?" asked Dolores.

Everyone leaned in, even the old guys, as we waited on Tanya to reveal the truth.

"I'll never tell," she said snidely. "And that means you can't prove a thing. I could have been lying just to wind you up."

"It's too late for that," said Dolores. "You confessed, and that means you'll confess again at the station."

"Maybe I won't," she said, petulant.

"I know how she did it," I sighed.

"You do?" asked Min. "How?"

"Frogs."

"Frogs?" everyone chorused.

Tanya blanched, and I knew I was right.

"Frogs," I confirmed.

"Why is everyone saying that lately?" asked Ronnie.

"Gav's really into tribal stuff, especially in South America," I said. "The motorhome was full of books as well as items he'd picked up on his travels. I'm not saying he had his entire collection there, but enough to get me to thinking. It's why I thought it was him for a while. My guess is that at his house you'll discover quite a few things he shouldn't have. Things that you shouldn't take from one country to another. Possibly arrowheads, ancient artifacts, and lots of live creatures too."

"Gav and his wife love exotic animals," said Ronnie.

"That's why I argued with him," admitted Stu. "Harper and I hate that people keep animals in confined spaces. It isn't right. We got into a fight about it."

"Right, and I'm guessing he's illegally imported things like frogs. The tiny ones. The natives of some regions in South America use them to poison the tips of darts. I looked it up. If you ingest it, you can die pretty much straight away from heart failure. It's very fast-acting. My guess is that Tanya got her hands on the frogs or the poison and used it. It's not something we'd ever look for when testing for poison in this country, especially in a pub full of pickles."

"Why, you sneaky little..." began Ronnie

"Yes, that's quite enough!" interrupted Dolores. "Is this true?"

"Yeah. Gav isn't a great guy, actually. Stu's right. He keeps these poor creatures in less than ideal conditions, and he even has the poisons of quite a few. I went around there when I knew nobody was home and stole some. It was easy to inject it into the onions and put some in the sandwiches. Stupid idiot should have eaten his sandwich and this would have worked perfectly."

Dolores nodded to me, then turned to Tanya and read her rights slowly.

"Why did you use a phone signal jammer?" I asked, the one piece of the puzzle that still didn't make sense.

"Because it was fun," she sneered.

"Fun?" raged Ronnie. "You thought it was fun? Just how insane are you, Tanya? How did you think you could get away with any of this?"

Tanya just shrugged. "Yes, Ronnie, fun. I figured it would confuse everyone if something went wrong, but also ensure nobody could get help from paramedics. It worked too."

The police took her away and we were left facing two very annoyed bowls players, staring forlornly at their green then at us like it was our fault. We got out of there as fast as we could before they had us levelling the green and reseeding.

Dolores joined us back at the campsite where nobody knew quite what to do. Ronnie and Meat retired to the pub while Stu and Harper went to put the kettle on in their motorhome—a cuppa was needed before they hit the road.

"How could Gav have got his hands on poison like that?" asked Min. "That's totally illegal, isn't it?"

"Absolutely," said Dolores. "I'll look into it, but he's in severe trouble. Not only for owning it, but we'll check about the conditions of the animals he has too. What's more problematic for him is that he had deadly poisons but didn't think to tell us even when people were dying. He must have linked the deaths with his collection. If not, then he's pretty dumb. But either way, he's got a lot to answer for."

"I'm assuming that's why he was so quiet when all this happened. Worried it might come back to him. I wouldn't be surprised if you don't find anything at his home now. Maybe he got his wife to dispose of it all."

"No, I think he truly didn't connect the two and he'll still have his collection. But we'll tie up the loose ends, don't you worry. I need to go, but I just wanted to have a word before I do. You did a good job, Max, and I'm not going to berate you for solving this before us. Being in the thick of things often means you discover little clues that we never can, and you picked up on things that we didn't. Well done."

"Um, thank you. I was expecting to be told off. That's usually what happens."

"I'm just grateful this is over. We were looking for the culprit in all the wrong places, and the jubilee was never a consideration, but it makes sense. Part of me is happy that Tanya will never get to inherit the money, if she ever gets out of prison, but Gav's daughter is a lovely lady and I've met her a few times. It would have been nice if her children got to have that money for their future, but I guess that's the way of the world." Dolores shrugged, then with a warm smile for us both she left.

Min, Anxious, and I watched her go, then stood, not knowing what to do now.

"That was intense," said Min, beaming at me.

"It was wild at the end, yes," I said, feeling strange.

"What's wrong?"

"I just feel bad for everyone. Ronnie's pub is shut, Tanya has ruined her life, and other people's, and although Gav might not be such a nice guy, his grandchildren, when they arrive, could have had a great future."

"But they would have never got the money anyway," Min reminded me. "The numbers wouldn't have added up, so things are no different now."

"I guess you're right."

"Max, you did an incredible thing. You figured this mess out, you saved a life by stopping Tanya, and you gave everyone the peace they needed. My hero." Min pecked me on the cheek and took my hands. "I don't know how you do it, but you did."

"Cup of tea?" called Harper from across the field.

With our work here done, we went to have a cuppa before deciding what to do next.

Chapter 20

Min left the next morning, promising to be in touch soon. Anxious and I were both sorry to see her go, but she had her own life and a job that she now loved. So we waved her off, then spent the day sorting out the campervan and helping Ronnie and Meat finish getting the pub cleaned up.

With Tanya out of the picture, there was plenty to keep us busy, and by the afternoon the pub was looking like it always had, but with one thing missing. Any customers.

Ronnie got a call while we were wiping down the bar, and when he finished he was beaming.

"What's made you so happy?" I asked.

"I've got the green light. Now we know nobody's going to kill the customers, I can open again. The only problem is I have no chef, and no staff to serve drinks. We can't handle it all on our own." Ronnie smiled at me as he raised an inquisitive eyebrow.

"Don't even ask," I warned.

"Max, just for a few days until I can get a new chef and barmaid. Please? It would really help me out."

"No way. I told you, that was the last time I work in a kitchen again. I don't want the stress, Ronnie, and I won't do it."

"Fair enough," he sighed.

"Why don't you teach me then?" asked Meat. "I'm pretty capable in the kitchen, but I need a few pointers."

"You want to be the chef?" asked Ronnie.

"Sure. I helped out Dexter, you know that, but being the chef would be fun. I like it. I can cook, I'm just not good at the other stuff. Figuring out what to order and when, and I don't understand how the system works for when you get the timing right for meals."

"I can teach you that. As long as I don't have to cook, I'll show you the rest. It's straightforward once you get the hang of it."

"Then it's a deal! Max, you do that for me and you can eat for free the entire time you're here. Free beer too. I'll open tonight, just for drinks, and in a few days we can get the kitchen up and running again. Meat, you sure?"

"I want to be a proper part of the team, Ronnie. No more just doing a bit of this and that. We need to get this place better organised."

"Yeah, you're right. Okay, then let's get to it!"

Two days later, I was done showing Meat how to run the kitchen. He was a surprisingly fast learner, and the food he produced was excellent. Once he understood how to time the orders and keep track of the stock levels, he was all set. Ronnie brought in new people to help him, plus a barmaid, and the pub was a constant hive of activity as deliveries were made, the freezer was re-stocked, and slowly customers began to return.

His old friends from the village came several times to help out, and Harry the florist festooned the place with fresh flowers, free of charge.

I managed to catch up on some much needed cooking of my own, but exclusively in my outdoor kitchen, refusing to make anything in the pub. It felt like returning home. One-pot cooking and plenty of time to relax in my chair and just watch the world go by. Time to reflect, to relax, and think about my life and the time I'd spent with Min. I was glad she'd come, happy she was now safe, and pleased we remained such great friends. Yes, the future was uncertain, but we had something special, which was a true blessing. I would do everything in my power to hold on to that.

The grand re-opening of the kitchen was a roaring success, and Meat surpassed himself, making excellent pub grub that went down a treat with the locals and those who had begun to arrive for the golden jubilee.

On the morning of my last day, as I had just finished stowing the sun shelter and was sitting in my camping chair with a cuppa before hitting the road, Ronnie and Meat came over to say their goodbyes.

"What are you looking so pleased about?" I asked Meat, the broad smile on his blunt face not something I had seen before. Normally about as emotional as a rock, he was almost bursting with excitement.

"Can I tell him?" Meat asked Ronnie.

"Sure, why not?" said Ronnie, his own smile spreading across his tanned face.

"Someone died in the village."

"Um, and that's good?" I asked, nonplussed.

"A poor old guy who'd been in hospital for months. Real sick like. He passed. Isn't that great?"

"If you say so. Doesn't sound good to me."

"He was very ill, and it was his time," said Ronnie. "Sometimes it's better to be done with things when there's no hope. He's at peace now."

"I guess you're right."

"And that's not all," squealed Meat, hopping from one foot to the other.

"Do you need to pee?" I asked.

"No. There's even better news," said Meat.

"Better than a man dying?" I asked, trying not to sound too sarcastic.

Meat was oblivious, and gushed, "Yeah. Loads better. Gav's daughter gave birth! To twins! So now they get the money. It's the golden jubilee today, so it worked out perfectly. Isn't that amazing?"

"It is. That's good news, guys. Do you know her?"

"Yeah, she's a real sweetie, and she deserves a break. Her and the babies are doing well, and apparently they're going to make an appearance at the jubilee in the village. It'll be a cracker of a day, Max."

"I bet it will. So, the numbers worked out in the end? That's incredible."

"There's more," declared Meat, now beside himself with excitement, his smile contagious.

"Oh, do tell," I laughed. Ronnie caught my eye and winked, amused by Meat's obvious joy.

"Tanya's grandfather is giving his share to the newborns. Ronnie got a call from him and he said that he's so upset about what Tanya did that there's no way he wants her to inherit, so he's offered it to the little uns. That means they don't have to split their share, but they get the lot between them. They'll be set up for a good future now, and that's such a nice thing to do. Isn't it wonderful?"

"Wonderful?" asked Ronnie with a frown. "I've never heard you use that word in your life. You usually say bloody great, or, crackin', now things are wonderful?"

"Yes, Ronnie, because they are," lectured Meat. "I'm done with playing the tough guy to impress the punters. From now on I'm all happiness and light and giving little children lollipops." Meat nodded to me, then wandered back to the pub, whistling as he went.

"I don't know what's got into him. Ever since he took over in the kitchen, it's like he's a different person."

"He's found his true calling, Ronnie. He's happy. Let him enjoy it."

"I will. And he's been much better company. I hadn't realised he was feeling like a spare wheel. Now he's a proper part of this place, and it's nice to see him happy. You sticking around for the jubilee? The village is looking awesome, and there's going to be a massive party. You should come to see the big reveal. They've got those oversized cheques to hand out and everyone's stoked about it. It's down to you, Max. You made this happen. You saved the day and you saved the village."

"I think I'll pass, but thanks. It's time for us to leave. We're heading back to the coast, maybe stop off on the way, and to be honest I'm shattered."

"Suit yourself. But I have something that might make you change your mind."

"Oh, what's that?" I was intrigued, but doubted he could sway me.

"There's a massive pickled onion eating competition. Even bigger than the one we had. And free pickles for all."

"Then I'll definitely pass."

"Thought you might," laughed Ronnie. "Well, thanks for everything, Max. You saved the village, you saved my pub, and you definitely saved me from a right pickle." Ronnie chortled at his own joke.

I groaned, and Anxious put his paws over his ears where he lay beside me.

"See you around, Ronnie," I said as I stood and we shook hands.

"Yeah, see you around, Max." Ronnie returned to the pub; the doors banged shut behind him.

I folded up my camping chair, rinsed out my mug, then stood outside Vee and smiled.

It might not have been a happy ending for everyone, but for those that deserved one, it had worked out just fine.

The End

But you know that isn't the case just yet. Read on for another incredible one-pot wonder (plus a bonus pickle recipe), and for news of what happens next for Max and Anxious as they hit the road yet again. **Vetted for Violence** finds them inexplicably drawn into their wildest, and most dangerous, adventure yet.

Recipe

Sunday Roast

Poor Max certainly had his one-pot wonders interrupted by all the poisoning. But don't let that put you off, because here's what he cooked up for himself and Anxious once a very perplexing pickle was solved.

No matter the weather, there's a British staple that cannot be beaten. The Sunday Roast. Yum! Pubs up and down the country do a roaring trade every Sunday serving their own version of this stalwart, but there's a bit of a cheat if you're short of pans, on the road, or fancy sitting around a campfire and relaxing whilst beautiful aromas tickle your taste buds.

How about a slow-cooked, one-pot Sunday Dinner? It may not have all the fancy trimmings, but the star of the show here is a fine cut of meat and some nice, soft potatoes that have soaked up all the amazing juices. To crisp them up, remove all the liquid at the end of cooking and let the heat from the cast-iron pan crisp up these babies until they're how you like them. Keep an eye on things, though.

Enjoy!

Ingredients

- A nice tightly rolled piece of brisket-around 3lb / 1.5kg
- Flour – 2 tbsp
- Rapeseed or sunflower oil – 1 tbsp
- Butter - a hefty knob

- A couple of peeled and halved carrots
- Two onions, peeled and quartered
- Two celery sticks, halved
- Three garlic cloves, peeled
- Beef, chicken, or vegetable stock - 1 pint / 500ml
- A big glass of red wine
- Seasoning - salt, pepper, a sprig of thyme, and a few bay leaves
- Six Maris Piper potatoes, halved
- English mustard – 1 tsp

Method

You will need a large casserole/dutch oven or similar with a well fitting lid.

- Start by pre-heating your casserole on a medium high heat while you prepare the brisket. Pat it dry, season with sea salt and pepper, then dust all over with a tablespoon or so of flour.
- Once the casserole is really hot add the oil and butter. As soon as you've got a good sizzle on, add the beef. You want to sear it all over so it gets a good golden colour with a few gnarly crunchy bits too.
- Turn the heat down to medium and add all the veg except the potatoes. Give it all a good stir round, add the stock, herbs, and wine, then let it bubble away to deglaze the sticky bits at the bottom.
- Add the lid, turn the heat down to a low simmer, and let it blip away slowly for about two hours.

- Now add the potatoes, give it a good stir, and continue to slowly simmer for another hour or so until the beef is tantalisingly soft and the potatoes are cooked through.

This is the point where you will need another pot/bowl/plate. Just for a bit! A spare skillet would suit the potatoes, too, but that really is cheating the one-pot theme. It all depends how well-stocked your van kitchen cupboards are and how much you want your potatoes to be golden. You could just serve it as it is for a delicious but slightly wetter dinner, or do as I do...

- Take out the brisket and fish out most of the vegetables (keeping the potatoes to one side). Cover to keep warm while you sort out your tasty gravy and melting potatoes.
- Pour the broth into a jug and whisk in some mustard and the rest of the flour if needed.
- Pop the potatoes back into your casserole with another knob of butter on a high heat to crisp up. They won't be roasted, but they will be buttery and golden and delicious.

Start plating up with the potatoes. That way the gravy can go back in the casserole for a few minutes to bubble up and ensure any floury taste is a thing of the past.

Bonus Recipe-English Pickled Onions

Christmas is not complete without English pickled onions. They need to mature for at least six weeks before eating.

Pickling is a serious endeavour. If you can enlist the help of others, the laborious peeling will be much more enjoyable. Please note your local food preservation and canning guidelines. This is how I make great pickles but you do yours.

Ingredients

- Pickling onions - 2lb / 1kg
- Salt - 4oz / 110g
- Malt vinegar - 1.5 pints / 750ml
- Sugar - 1 tbsp
- Dried red chillies - 4
- Mustard seeds - 1 tsp
- Coriander seeds - 1 tbsp
- Black peppercorns - 1 tsp
- Ginger - 2 inch piece sliced
- Bay leaves - 4

Method

- Your first job is to peel the onions. The easiest way to do this is to slice off both ends then place the onions in a large bowl. Cover with boiling water and leave to stand for five minutes. The softened skin should come off easily with a small sharp knife.

- Place your peeled onions in a clean bowl and cover with cold water. Drain this into a pan, add the salt, and warm slightly to dissolve it.

- Once cooled, pour the brine over the onions. You need them to be completely submerged so place a plate inside the top of the bowl and weigh it down. Leave to stand somewhere cool for 24 hours.

- Now you make your spiced pickling vinegar (you can buy ready-made but that's not nearly as interesting). Place the vinegar in a large pan. Wrap the remaining ingredients (except the bay leaves) in a piece of muslin (or spice bag) and drop that into your pan along with the bay leaves. Bring the vinegar to the boil and simmer for five minutes then remove from the heat. Cover and leave to infuse overnight.

- The next day, fish the spice bag out of the vinegar and drain the onions from their salty bath and pat dry (don't rinse them though). Pack them tightly into sterilised jars. You can add some of the spices from the vinegar (not the ginger though) and cover with the vinegar. I like to add a chilli or two to each jar, but beware they do get hotter. If there is any spiced vinegar left (there always is), keep it in a sealed jar to use in future pickling projects.

- This is the bit where you should refer to your own government's food preservation and canning guidelines and follow their expert advice.
- I do it the old fashioned British way: Seal the jars (non metallic lids so we don't get any crazy chemistry happening with the acidic vinegar), and store in a cool, dark place for at least six weeks before enjoying.

From the Author

What a pickle! At least Max managed to save the day once again. Continue Max's Campervan Case Files in <u>Vetted for Violence.</u> Things get wild when Anxious is poorly and has to visit THE DOCTOR. No, don't say it out loud!

Be sure to <u>stay updated about new releases</u> and fan sales. You'll hear about them first. No spam, just book updates at www.authortylerrhodes.com

You can also <u>follow me on Amazon</u> https://www.amazon.com/stores/author/B0BN6T2VQ5

<u>Connect with me on Facebook</u> https://www.facebook.com/authortylerrhodes/

Printed in Great Britain
by Amazon